# The Amsterdam Confessions of a Shallow Man

Simon Woolcot

Copyright © 2013 Simon Woolcot

All rights reserved.

ISBN-978-1493595969

# DEDICATION

To Anneke for all the support.
To Jack for being the best friend a man ever had.

# CONTENTS

# ACKNOWLEDGMENTS

Laura Van Stelten,
Notonlycooking.com

Abuzer Van Leeuwen from the Dutchreview.com
Wendy Deun from Designopzolder.com for the logo and book cover

# INTRODUCTION

Anna, a blonde bombshell of a woman from the beautiful city of Frankfurt, who is one of my best friends, my colleague and who claims to know me better than I know myself, says that I am the shallowest man she's ever known, and that because I constantly deny being so, the best way for me to realize quite how lacking in any real depth I am would be to start writing down exactly how I live my life for a month. Her theory is that I'm so busy living my allegedly shallow existence, that only when seeing my activities written down will it dawn on me how I am the living equivalent of a worm's grave, i.e. extremely shallow.

A month is a hell of a long time, most of my relationships don't last that long (joking) and I'm not too happy about making such a long term commitment, but since Anna claims that I lack the discipline to keep a diary, I am intent on proving her wrong. So welcome to the diaries of Simon Woolcot, an allegedly spoiled and shallow Expat from London living in Amsterdam.

# BOOK 1 THE BOOK OF LUST

# JUNE 28TH

The iPhone alarm woke me up with the soothing sounds of John Coltrane's version of Nature Boy. I have an Alarm App that allows me to select which song I'll wake up to. It also chooses the right time to wake me up based on sleep cycles. This prevents me from being shocked awake and - because I love Coltrane's music- starts my day the right way.

Proceeded to my ensuite bathroom. While looking in the mirror, what did I see? More hair in my ears. This is the bain of my existence. No sooner is ear hair removed that it comes sprouting back like weed in some uncared for garden. I've noticed that since turning 40 unless I pay due attention I could grow an Afro on my ears. So I reached out for the ear clippers and gave it a good trim, ditto for the nose hair. Jumped into the shower and applied my Biotherm Homme facial scrub, while also using liberal amounts of my Chanel Allure shower gel. Say what you like about Coco Chanel (alleged Nazi collaborator, raider of the minibar in the Paris Ritz Hotel during the war) but she knew how to put together a damn good shower gel.

Hopped out of the shower and applied plenty of Vichy body lotion, pricey but worth every penny. One of the first things I do when spending the night at a new love interest's apartment is to check out the shower gel and body lotion choices. All you need to know about a woman is in her bathroom cabinet. I've made my excuses and left a girl's place faster than a Dutchman bending over to pick up a dropped coin due to the lady of the moment's bathroom cabinet contents. Had a shave, applied face cream (Chanel of course), hand lotion, deodorant (have a guess), brushed my teeth and then headed to the spare room which also doubles as a walk-in closet.

Spent some time selecting the right suit, shirt and tie combination for work. I'm an IT Director at McCulloch Management Consultants and looking sharp is as important, if not more critical, than the work I do. I have 15 tailor made suits and over 50 shirts that I can wear for work. To ensure that I don't repeat the same combinations too often, I keep an Excel spreadsheet that notes which suits were worn with which shirts and ties on which day. My rule is never to repeat the same combination within a single month. Went for the worsted grey with dark blue shirt and pink/blue tie combination, last worn on May 27th. Excellent!

For a change of pace, I took a bus to work. One of the great things about living in Amsterdam is the public transport. I walk for 10 minutes from my apartment overlooking the Sarphartipark to Museumplein and from there take the bus to our office which takes 20 minutes. I stand the whole way, even though it's possible to have a seat, as I don't want any muck from the great unwashed getting on my lovingly dry-cleaned suits. The Dutch public are the worst dressed people in Europe and I'm from the UK so that's really saying something.

You want to talk about culture shock? Well it seems here that:

1. Judging by the color combinations they wear, most people appear to dress in the dark to save electricity.
2. There must be a law that forces people to wear jeans with everything.
3. Women seem to think it's acceptable to leave the house with hair that is still wet and glistening like the body of a wet rat.

Spotted the usual fashion disasters on the bus, always good to help shock one completely awake.

Spent a fairly typical day at work, with the "thank God it's Friday" feeling running through my veins. Friday is what we guys at work call "Green Card night". This means that those poor specimens who live with partners and usually have to beg their better halves for permission to leave the house are given the permission to go out and have a civilized (ho, ho, ho) evening with me, who definitely does not have a woman to answer to.

Friday night is a bit of a blur. Started out in the company bar. McCulloch goes against Dutch society rules by having women who by and large do dress very well. We're a British partnership with offices in over 20 countries and our Amsterdam office is pretty international, with 30% of the 700 employees not being from the Netherlands. I'm sure that the Dutch women who work for us can't wait to get home and get out of their smart business wear, mess up their hair and stick on a pair of old jeans with a top that doesn't match. Anyway, after some pointless flirting with some of the ladies in the office bar I headed to an Eetcafe

(brasserie) which, as coincidence would have it, is a three-minute walk from my apartment.
Along for the night out came Richard, another 40 something Brit who I've worked with for years. Richard is 165 cm tall, smartly dressed, a SAP expert who has a thing for black women. His current partner doesn't trust me at all and dislikes him hanging out with me, no idea why, really. Also along is Nathanial, 35-year-old Expat from Toronto. He looks like an American footballer and is a gentle giant. The best way to annoy him is to ask where in the US he comes from! If you look up the term "pussy-whipped' in a Thesaurus his name and address appear instead of the explanation. The poor sap married his former Dutch secretary, the leggy, skinny (but badly dressed) Haike, who now organizes his private life with savage efficiency. He generally attends the Friday night get-together about once every six to eight weeks due to Haike booking out his social life with endless visits to her parents and other relatives. Like I said, poor sap.

Our token Dutch friend, Koen is an excellent Project Manager and all round party animal. He lives in Den Haag, which is a good 1.5 hours travelling each way daily, but it works for him as property prices there are much cheaper than in Amsterdam. This matters for a man with a fast growing family. He's the father of three kids and claims (unusually for a Dutchman) that he wears the trousers at home and is not bossed around by his partner.

Anna, the reason I'm writing this diary, also came along. So, as well as a token Dutchman, we also had a token female. Anna is 185 cm tall, blonde, has (at least as far as I can see) spectacular breasts and dresses in what I would describe as a crisply efficient manner, usually in simple elegant business suits at work (she's an in-house lawyer) and dark trousers and matching shirts outside of it. I've known Anna for years. I once did a one-year assignment in our Frankfurt office. She politely but firmly rebuffed my attempts to make a pass at her and we became good friends, which we remain to this day. Anna is 38, divorced and, in spite of what people say about Germans, has a wicked sense of humor. Actually it's often difficult to tell with her whether she's laughing with me or at me.

So we had a good meal at De Duvel and the night would have ended in a civilized fashion had we stayed there. Instead, someone (possibly me) suggested that we go onto the Palladium, a bar/club in the tourist center of Amsterdam, Leidesplein. Palladium is full of incredibly hot, ambitious women. By ambitious, I mean that most of them have a single goal, which is to meet a footballer or a guy who is wealthy and stupid enough to put up with them not working so that they can spend their days shopping and living off the guy's bank balance. Gold Digger central. This bar stands out as it is actually one of the few places in the country where women will actually bother to dress up in something other than jeans and (shockingly) not only wear make-up but do their hair properly as well.

Don't get me wrong; I have no issues with Gold Diggers as long as they realize that my goal is to get shot of them as quickly as possible.

So we drank, drank, danced and drank some more. Anna, who can't stand the Palladium, left us at De Duvel to have in-depth conversations about which women were the hottest and the never-ending debate regarding real versus silicone-enhanced boobies.

I vaguely remember walking up to a woman and saying to her "36DD." "I don't understand, what do you mean?" she asked me with a confused look on her face. "Well your T-shirt does say Guess."

It's amazing how well Dutch women can swear in English. Koen, having to travel the furthest, bailed out at the inappropriately early time of 12.30 am. Nathaniel received several control phone calls from his stricter half, who then ordered him home around 1 am. Richard, being a British real man and hardcore like myself stayed on till at least 3 am. He bravely refused to answer numerous calls from his woman who no doubt wanted to order him home as well. We then stupidly went on to another bar where we left as merry as investment bankers at bonus time and I wandered the streets alone back to the Woolcot palace. Richard, who lives in Jordaan headed off in the direction of the Red Light district. I have hazy memories of how I got home.

# HOW TO GET RICH IN THE NETHERLANDS

If you want to get rich in the Netherlands, there are two guaranteed ways to do so.

1. Open a bakery.
2. Invent a spread to put on bread.

You may wonder why I suggest these two options. The Dutch are the largest consumers of bread and things to put on bread on planet Earth and probably beyond. If you walk into any supermarket you will see an entire aisle dedicated to all manner of things to add onto bread. The creativity on display here is amazing: chocolate or forest fruit flavoured flakes (really), Mexican, tomato, cucumber and many other exotic acquired taste spreads.

The Dutch take their sandwich flavours seriously. Go to the sandwich spread section of any supermarket and you'll see flavour connoisseurs acting as if they are choosing fine wine in a Bordeaux vineyard. "Shall I choose peanut butter, chocolate flakes or a Mexican Heinz Sandwich spread?" Decisions, decisions. Forget investing in stocks, invent a sandwich spread with a flavour that no normal person would ever think of and sell it in the Netherlands. It will make you rich. Lekker!!

# JUNE 29$^{TH}$

Saturdays are pure stress. Woke up, or shall I say got out of bed at 1pm. I think when I got home I tried to watch some porn that I'd downloaded a couple of days before but much to my disgust was American. Nothing against the people of the USA. Love the country and its people but what appalling porn! American porn reflects what I find to be the incredible optimism of the country, as well as the never-ending goal for bigger things. American porn "actresses" don't just have breasts, they have huge silicone enhanced bazookas that can turn round corners ahead of their owners. They don't just have orgasms, they scream the place down at the top of their voices even before the actors touch them. No wonder Americans need such big houses; it's to shield the noise they make during sex.

Anyway, gave up on the film, staggered to bed. Woke up hangover free due to the Simon Woolcot patented hangover avoidance method: one glass of alcohol followed by one glass of water. Works a treat.

Saturdays are always stressful, had to struggle with some major decisions:

1. Where to eat breakfast?
2. PlayStation for a couple of hours or breakfast first?
3. Where to go shopping?
4. Should I go on another date with Irina?
5. Pick up dry cleaning before or after shopping?

Did options 1 and 2 together; simply had a bowl of muesli while playing Call of Duty Black Ops for what turned out to be two hours. Then took a visit to my Tailors, who are in my humble opinion the best clothes shop in Amsterdam if not in the country. The Tailors only sell clothes for men and I normally avoid the shop on a Saturday as it's full of badly dressed women telling their men what clothes they should be selecting, oh the irony. But as it was in the general direction of the P.C. Hooftstraat shopping street, the area where I had planned to do some shopping, I thought I'd look in. P.C. Hooftstraat is the equivalent of Rodeo Drive in Beverly Hills, Bond Street in London and the Rue St Honorare in Paris. It's the center of exclusive boutiques and brands. Armani, Louis Vuitton and, yes,

Chanel all have stores in this street, to name but a few.
My Tailors was packed out with hen-pecked men and their dominant women, so I left and headed for a bit of window shopping.

Visited Irina, my 34-year-old occasional, incredible, aerobic and intense regular Russian shag. My relationship with Irina could be simply described as: I take her to fabulous restaurants and pick up the bill; in return she shags me within two inches of my life. 177 cm, jet-black hair, a good line of exotic lingerie and skintight dresses make Irina a joy to be with. We've been seeing each other on and off since last October and we are supposed to have a no-hassle, no-commitment relationship which suits me perfectly but of course these things never last as planned.

Upon arriving at her pokey apartment on the first floor of a building with a steep, moth-eaten carpet-covered stairway, I waited for her to open her front door with a sense of excitement. In the past she has often greeted me only wearing a pair of high-heeled shoes, or with racy underwear. I was to be disappointed as she was fully dressed in a tight off-the-shoulder black dress cut diagonally across her shapely legs.

I went to give her my usual greeting of a passionate kiss, but she only turned and offered me her cheeks, sadly the ones on her face. She then strutted across her apartment, which gave me the opportunity to take in her hourglass figure and how the dress clung to her arse that was definitely at the top of the Beyoncé Knowles league table of hot backsides.

"Have some wine, Simon," she said motioning towards the dining table, where an already open bottle of Pinot Grigio stood with two glasses.

"Is everything OK with you, honey?" I asked. "You seem a little frosty today."

"Sure, why would everything not be OK? I am alone here in Amsterdam, with no family, not many friends. My bitch of a boss hates me, always criticizes my work, my English. I stay in the office sometimes till 9 at night. Does she care? Does she say 'thank you, Irina, for working so hard'? No, she just negative, negative, negative all the time. I have so much to give work, but she brings me down."

On and on she whined, as if I don't have enough of my own problems to deal with and instead I want to listen to hers. Pretending to give a shit, I opened my arms and said: "My poor sweetheart, come here, let me give you a hug."

She melted into my arms and I hugged her hot body closely against mine, at which point my cock sprang to life. She pulled away from me faster than a Dutch person that's been asked to leave a tip at a restaurant.

"Why we make only the sex? Why we no spend more time together?" She looked at me with enquiring eyes as she said this. Her voice took on a woeful tone.

"We can't only fuck. No get me wrong, I love to fuck with you, but I'm not just your whore, you must treat me like lady."

"Don't I treat you well?" I responded. "We're not exactly eating Kebabs and Burgers, are we?" Trying not to laugh, she replied, "Yes, that is true but you never take me to meet friends, we just fuck and eat, eat and fuck." "Try fucking with the intensity that we have without eating," I said to her. "Believe me, it wouldn't be as good or as long. Sweetheart, you know that what we have is hot and good fun, and I just want to keep it the way it is."

Fixing me with an intense stare, she said, "You want to keep fuck me when you are horny, then eating, then fucking, then fuck some more, with no future for anything more, is that what you want?"

I couldn't have summed it up any better. "At least for now, let's just see how things go, but I'm not promising anything. We have a good time, don't we? Let's just allow things to develop naturally." Sighing deeply, she responded, "I'm a lady, I'm getting older, I can't live like this forever."

The conversation definitely set alarm bells ringing, but not having vigorous intense sex with her is something I'm not prepared to do at the moment. For a start I'd have to go to the gym more often to make up for the thousands of calories I'd not be burning during our intense sessions. I admit to having a definite weakness for Russian women. In my experience, they are usually incredibly feminine, with painted finger nails, Stiletto heels, tight outfits that display their bodies and (something extremely rare in this age of feminism) they are actually usually not against cooking for their men as well. Win/Win.

As if to prove my point, she growled at me, "I know what you want, you horny bastard." She then pulled up her dress to reveal a lack of underwear, and then bent over the dining table, where I proceeded to fuck her to a shuddering climax. I made a mental note to make sure never to eat at that table, then, following a shower, we jumped into a taxi and headed off to dinner.

Had dinner at one of my favorite one star Michelin places, the Vinkeles in the Dylan Hotel. My rule is: single Michelin star places for occasional shags and exceptionally hot dates and two stars if I'm in an actual relationship, so I spend most of my time visiting one star establishments. Vinkeles is a stunning place, beautiful décor, dark, sexy, with (amazingly for the Netherlands) excellent service and fine contemporary cuisine. I love good food and I often bring different dates there. The Maître d' welcomed me by name with a knowing smile at me being there again with another stunning looking woman. Had an exceptional meal for an eye-watering price. Of course Irina didn't even attempt to offer to contribute to the bill, after all she would be providing dessert.

# JEANS: ALMOST MANDATORY IN THE NETHERLANDS

One of the first things that I noticed upon moving to Amsterdam was how almost everyone wears jeans. I've seen people wearing jeans at weddings, funerals, posh restaurants, in nice bars, clubs… Actually it's difficult to think of an occasion where people don't wear jeans. It's as if a law has been passed insisting that people must wear jeans at all times during evenings and weekends.

When getting dressed for a night out, the thought process in the Netherlands appears to be: "Which jeans shall I wear this evening?"

When out and about in Amsterdam, looking at all the people in jeans is like passing through the Valley of the Clones. Why wear a nice jacket or designer blouse only to wear a pair of old jeans with it? I understand that most people cycle and it's also a matter of comfort and a practical thing, but there are things other than jeans that can be worn. This is a plea to all the pretty young and not-so- young things going out in Amsterdam and elsewhere this evening. Leave the jeans at home, just this once. Go on, try it! You know you can do it.

# JUNE 30$^{TH}$

Spent most of the night and morning being worked out on by Irina. The sheer intensity of sex with that woman is like running a half marathon while being chased by a Rottweiler. An incredible night, her bedside talents never fail to amaze and exhaust me. Escaped from her clutches at 11.30. She left me with a parting statement of: "Why you go always? We must spend time together, not only for the sex."

Alarm bells were ringing louder and louder. It's always a relief to be leaving her badly lit, pokey apartment which has a faint musty smell I can't quite put my finger on. The person who invented the saying "not enough room to swing a cat" was obviously a former lover of Irina's. Whenever I'm at her place, I'm always bumping into bits of furniture because of the compact layout and the need to maximize the use of space in her studio apartment. Irina lives on the Vijzelstraat, which is about 15 minutes walking distance from my place and is pretty centrally located. This is why she pays a staggering 1350 Euros a month for a place which smells like it would after attempting to swing the cat, that had been buried under the floorboards for good measure.

Had just enough time for a shower and a quick change of clothes before going to meet Anna for lunch.

Anna lives in the next street to me and when we are both in town we usually have lunch or dinner together on Sundays. We met at my local Café, De Duvel. The place was packed out with an assortment of local yuppies, students, yuppies with kids and with a small smattering of clueless tourists who, even though they had an English menu, were looking at the contents as if it were written in Cyrillic.

Being late as I was, Anna had already found a table for two near the entrance and motioned to her watch as I approached. After the obligatory Dutch style greeting of three kisses on the cheeks I sat down. She looked at me curiously up and down and said, "Hi, you look exhausted."

"Well, you know me; I've been working out a lot and running of course."

"Working out? Is that what they call it now?"

"I have no idea what you mean, I'm a sporty kind of guy, have to keep the temple known as my body in shape, so that's why I'm tired."

"Simon, you look tired from the kind of sport that doesn't involve gyms or running. Look at your eyes and the way you are sitting, you want to go back to bed, don't you?"

"Is that an offer? I thought you'd never ask". Rolling her eyes she said, "Come on, be serious, what have you been up to, you naughty boy?" "Anna, my suspicious token hot female friend, I'm as innocent as a politician caught fiddling their expenses." "Of course you are," she replied, with the emphasis on the 'Of course.' "So what did you do yesterday evening, and was any Russian involved?" "I had a civilized evening with Irina."

"Natuerlich" she replied triumphantly. "So, that explains the red eyes and the body that looks as if it's in pain. Was she hard on you? Fitness Russian style, looks tiring." She laughed at me rather than with me.

Slowly sipping on a Latte I replied, "What you forget, my judgmental Fraeulein, is that it's not so long ago that people used to marry just so they could have sex; now that's shallow."

"At least I make it clear, well I should say reasonably, no, fairly clear that I'm not looking for a serious relationship and just want to have a good time. Look at the divorce rates in the UK, 50%, that's loads of people who would have been better off just having regular sex and not spoiling it by making a commitment and getting married."

"You only think this way because of what happened with Lucy," she replied with a probing stare.

At the mention of my poisonous ex I changed the subject. I asked her about her love life, but she is (of course) very discreet, and getting information out of her is like trying to teach a parrot to quote the works of Shakespeare. Eventually she told me that she'd had plenty of offers recently (no surprise there, you should see her) but had yet to meet anyone interesting.

"Interesting?" I asked. "Your problem is that, having gotten to know me, you'll never find any man who measures up to my standards." She laughed and said: "That is true, I don't think I'll ever meet anyone quite like you. You are definitely one of a kind."

Following a pretty mediocre lunch, which consisted of a chicken club sandwich served with a bowl of crisps of all things, Anna then tried to convince me to accompany her to the Van Gogh Museum. What is it with women and museums? I told her that I don't know any straight men that voluntarily go to museums and one of the great things about not being in a relationship is not being nagged into visiting such places. She repeated her point about me being shallow and then we headed our separate ways.

As I hadn't drunk any alcohol, I changed into my sports gear and went for my usual long Sunday run. Ran 19 kilometers very slowly. Considering the previous night's meal and intense sex in multiple positions, multiple times, that wasn't bad.

Headed afterwards to the gym, which is one of the most exclusive in Amsterdam, full of pretty young and not-so- young things, who seem to spend more time hanging around machines chatting very loudly, rather than doing any actual exercise. I get the impression that Dutch women have hearing problems, as instead of just talking they tend to shout at each other simultaneously. How they understand what is being said is beyond me.

Plenty of eye candy in my gym and I can forgive attractive women almost anything. No conversation between young women nowadays can take place without mentioning Facebook and WhatsApp. It pays to wear my Dr Dre Beats Studio headphones in the gym to drown this nonsense out.

I can forgive beautiful women almost anything. Not including my evil ex Lucy, who actually did some things that I could never forgive, but, that aside, as I said usually I'm full of forgiveness, depending on the looks of the recipient.

This diary-keeping thing is tough and thirsty work! Nothing much more to report about Sunday. Had a good nap, and then had some spicy green curry, delivered courtesy of an iPhone food home delivery app. Then did something that I'd been putting off all week, caught up on my Facebook account, which is a curse of the modern age and requires ever more time to deal with. Was thrilled to hear that Steven, a guy I went to school with in the seventies and eighties and who I haven't seen face to face since 1989, sent a message saying he is thinking of repainting his apartment. A woman who I'm not even sure how or why I friended is going to have kittens. I think she meant to say that her cat will have kittens, or (who knows) perhaps that is genuine exciting news, she is about to give birth to kittens. No doubt the father is called Tom. He's not one of my 285 Facebook friends. I should really cancel my account but it's like the Mafia, once you're in they don't let you leave.

The only positive thing I can say about Facebook is that it's good for keeping an index of morons. In the not-too- distant past you'd actually have to meet, work with or date someone before realizing that they are dumber than a troupe of mime artists. Now all you have to do is Google their Facebook profile and look out for the following indicators of being a moron:

Selfies, photos usually (but not always) taken by women of themselves, often in varying states of undress.

Huge amounts of personal details available on the profile that helpfully advise potential burglars not only of the exact address of where the profile owner lives, but also thoughtfully includes such essential details as when they are going on holiday, or (even better) live photos uploaded from the holiday with exciting commentary such as " Here's a photo I've taken of myself topless on the beach in Barcelona." "I'll be here for another week."

Lots of photos of the profile owner in fancy dress, drinking large amounts of alcohol and helpful images of them lying drunk on a sofa, in a gutter or with their heads over a toilet bowl after a good night out. Lovely.

My heart froze and hairs stood up all over my body seeing that I had a message from the psychopathic Lucy, an ex-girlfriend. She once used Facebook (or Stalkbook as it should be called) to send a message to two of her successors to ask what I had told them about her.

Lucy was the kind of girl who could start a fight with a nun and she could swear so fluently that even war veterans would burst into tears. The Dalai Lama would want to commit murder within ten minutes of meeting her. She had the kind of temper that would intimidate Mike Tyson. She was short, hot and aggressive. The first time I saw her she was snogging another woman in a bar, it was lust at first sight. What then followed were two years of Hell. Passionate hot sex, screaming arguments, break-ups, break-up sex, reunions, break-ups, broken plates, glasses, records, ripped clothes, damaged furniture, SMS terror, phone calls morning noon and night, tears, wailing, whining and pining. The Police were called several times, and all of our friends told us that we shouldn't be together, but just like junkies who continue to shoot heroin into their veins knowing full well it could kill them, we couldn't stop. We were so hot together that London burned in our wake. Birds would see us together, collapse and die on the spot. Hardened gangsters turned to God, blind men would scream, children would run crying for their mothers, plants would wilt in our presence; we were poison.

They say that an alcoholic is never really cured and I'm still afraid of what would happen if we were to see each other. Fortunately, she is now living in Melbourne. The UN intervened and said that it was for the good of mankind that we lived on different continents.

It's been eight years since we parted yet every time I hear from her my heart jumps. She sent me a message to say that she would be in Amsterdam on business for a week at the end of July. I didn't reply, will need to think very carefully about my next move.

Had some Thai food delivered for dinner, which burned like money in the pocket of a British stag party tourist in the Red Light District.

Watched some German porn, which is significantly superior to its silicone-loaded, multi-decibel orgasmic American counterpart. German porn, like Germans themselves, gets straight zur Sache (to the point): no nonsense sex with people who actually look like you could bump into them in your local Aldi, Beer Garden, or BMW dealership as opposed to in a plastic surgery clinic.

# AMSTERDAM – A PARADISE FOR SMOKERS

Most civilized countries (including the Netherlands) banned the smoking of cigarettes in bars and clubs years ago. However, the big difference in the Netherlands compared to most of its neighbors is the total lack of enforcement of the smoking laws in bars in Amsterdam.

The laws were brought in largely to protect both the employees and the customers of bars from the effects of passive smoking. Many a bar owner appears to have discovered scientific evidence that people are immune to the effects of cigarettes after 11 pm, when many bars suddenly allow people to smoke openly. Since Amsterdam has the highest number of smokers under the age of thirty, this is great news for tobacco companies, but not for those of us who don't appreciate coming home after a night out smelling like an ashtray.

The Shallow Man's response to this is to never date women who smoke. So obviously the city is full of broken hearted women who are considering giving up smoking due to the Shallow Man's lack of interest in them as a result of their filthy habit.

# JULY 1ST OR ENTER THE NERD

Faced one of life's eternal mysteries: why are there always odd socks? I'm constantly buying socks, only to have individual socks vanish. In Amsterdam it's common to have mice in apartments. While I've seen no evidence of any mouse infestation in my place, I can't help wondering if there is a gang of light-fingered mice sneaking into my place and stealing individual socks, perhaps to decorate their nests.

The cleaning lady comes on a Monday; she's a lady from Gambia, Zambia or somewhere in Africa. Sarah Palin apparently thought Africa was a country, not a continent. I understand her confusion. The cleaning lady whose name I can never remember claims to need five hours to clean my place and charges 50 Euros an hour for this service. I'm sure she's probably finished in less than two hours, then spends the rest of her time listening to my music or watching my DVD's, but since she does an excellent job of cleaning and ironing my shirts I can't complain.

At work a new colleague has joined our team from the London office. George is a forty-something network specialist. To call him a snake would be an insult to all reptiles. He's the kind of guy if you shake hands with whom you should check if your watch is still there afterwards. He'd have done exceptionally well back in the Roman times. I can just see him instilling intrigues and plots against Caesar, hanging out with Brutus, egging him on to overthrow the Emperor. He's been seconded to Amsterdam due to him possessing some skills that we urgently need at the moment, however I'll be installing multiple full-length mirrors in my office so that I can literally watch my back.

He's also a walking-talking-living cliché of an IT Person. Overweight, a real porker and (shockingly for an IT guy) a huge fan of Star Trek and science-fiction in general. Within ten minutes of meeting him this morning, he already managed to throw in several phrases that, to my embarrassment, I recognized from Star Trek. He immediately latched on to this seeing in me another potential "Trekkie," as fans of the series are called. It took far too long for me to get him out of my office. Only when I got up and walked out the room did he follow, quoting pieces from Star Trek on the way. He is what the Germans would describe as a *besser wisser*, in other words a complete know-it-all. He asked me how I get to the office, when I mentioned to him that I walk to Museumplein then take the bus or take an Uber taxi he immediately advised me that it would be quicker to take the number 5 tram and then change to take the 51 metro to Oudekerkerlaan. "You could save at least 20 minutes a day." This is him telling a man who has been living in Amsterdam for five years the fastest way to get to the office. He's the kind of guy that, if you discuss a film with him, will tell you the extended edition (which you of course haven't seen) was much better.

If you order a new gadget, he'll tell you that you could have got it for 25% less if you'd ordered it from a website that only he of course has ever heard of. Great start to the week having him around. He'll report to Remko, one of my direct reports, and I'll do my best to keep him at arm's length. Something that will be difficult to do as he is also an Olympic level arse kisser and never misses an opportunity to ingratiate himself with senior management. While I was enjoying a quick lunch with Anna in the canteen, not only did he come over, thus forcing me to introduce him, he then sat with us and bored me half to death with tales of his relocation hassles with Dutch bureaucracy. Anna at least appeared to find him amusing or (hopefully) she was just being polite. Realizing she was German, he then began to speak what I could only describe as pidgin German very loudly. He sounded like an old record with a scratch through the middle. Anna politely answered him in German; I then interceded and told him that we only had twenty minutes for lunch and that I had plans this evening, so didn't want to continue the discussion in German. He glowed as red as a beetroot and then switched to English. Just for a microsecond I caught a murderous flash in his eyes, but he then returned to his usual smarmy self. I've upset the serpent, better watch out.

Monday evening, much to my shock and amazement, Nathanial, who you'll recall is the most pussy-whipped man on the planet, was actually free from the clutches of his cloying, octopus-like wife, so he came round to my place, where we enjoyed an intellectual evening, eating take-out Turkish food and an intense PlayStation session of Pro Evolution Soccer, the only football computer game worth playing. Nat is a beer man, which is something I refuse to even have in the Woolcot Palace, so he had to make do with a 2001 Chateau Margeaux, from the Brane-Cantenac vineyard. The philistine had the cheek to complain and say that he would have preferred a beer. It's like feeding a Michelin Star meal to a dog. Of course I beat him easily, which is why it's always a pleasure on the rare occasions when we get together for a game or three. As his stricter half never lets him play computer games, his skills have deteriorated to a point that I can easily beat him; there was a time when he was shit hot on such things.

His lovely wife called him around 10.30 and ordered him home, as he had to work the next morning. "Does she write your name in your underpants as well?" I asked him.

"At least I have someone who cares that I get up in time."

"Really? Is that you what have her for? Take my advice and get yourself an iPhone Alarm App; easy to manage and it doesn't forbid you from going out with guys or tell you what time you need to get home, or how long you can stay on the PlayStation."

"You don't know what you're missing out on, man. There's nothing better than having someone who loves you being there with you every night, every morning, all the time."

"Stop now, Nat, you're turning my blood cold and I can feel the dinner coming; you don't want me to throw up, do you? Each to their own, but I'm glad that you're happy."

On that sentimental note, Nat headed home to the wife.

Watched the BBC news which is available on all good Dutch cable providers along with most of the BBC channels, something that I know annoys some of the locals as they feel that this discourages us lazy English-speaking Expats from learning more about the country we actually live in. Whenever this point is brought up by a Dutchman I always advise them to vote for Geert Wilders next time as I'm sure he'll have all non-Dutch speaking foreigners put in labor camps for the good of Dutch society and will have us wearing jeans, counting our money and messing up our hair in no time.

There were several messages from Lucy waiting for me on Facebook.

From Lucy
To: Simon

Why are you such a rude bastard?

How many messages do I have to send you to get a fucking response, you self-obsessed ignorant womanizing BASTARD!

I'm coming all the way from Australia and are you sooooo busy that you can't spare me one evening? What do you think I'm going to do after all this time? Rape you? I deserve the courtesy of an answer.

That's the least you can do after all the things you did to me back then.

From Simon
To: Lucy

Well, Hello to you. Glad to see you've learned to get your temper under control. After all these years you still think that yelling, shouting and swearing are appropriate at all times. I was planning to respond but, believe it or not, I do actually have other things to do apart from reading Facebook and replying to mad women. God, you really only have two modes, mad and outright crazy.

Let me think about it.

From Lucy
To: Simon

Prayer is the last refuge of the scoundrel, so I'm not surprised that you have to bring God into it, though I don't know why. God, if he lived, is as dead to you as he is to me. Money, career, wine, sex, those are your Gods as they are mine. You were also once mine and I yours, but you couldn't handle me. So you need time to think do you? Well FUCK OFF then.

# WHERE TO MEET AMBITIOUS WOMEN IN AMSTERDAM

If you're looking to meet ambitious women, the kind that set themselves clear goals and then set out to exceed them, my advice is to go to the Palladium restaurant and bar in Amsterdam. There you'll find women who actually wear lots of make-up, nice shoes and clothes and display themselves like dummies in a P.C. Hooftstraat shop window.

These women are not just looking for any run-of-the-mill man with a normal career, but have with single minded focus set their sights on footballers, gangsters or wealthy DJ's, bankers and property developers. The men in question should also preferably drive a Porsche, BMW, Mercedes or any other luxury car that's less than two to three years old; after all there has been a global recession.

As clusters of such women inhabit the bar, it often attracts not only footballers, DJ's and property dealers, etc but also men pretending to be such. Bottles of champagne are ordered and paid for with pin and credit cards in the shaking hands of the owners, who try and pretend not to be nervous as they mouth a silent prayer to their God hoping that the transaction will be accepted. Groups of men grudgingly share the cost of the champagne, which is then proudly put in the best spot of the table, strategically positioned to attract the attention of the gathered groups of women.

Much loud conversation is made by the men talking about their weekend homes in the south of France, how they had to pick up their cars from the Porsche dealership or the new Hublot watch that's on order but not yet arrived. Much posturing in the hope that some pretty, but cold and calculating not-so-young thing will suddenly show interest.

The men posture, the women pout and shout at each other as Dutch ladies are prone to do. When and if a woman shows interest in one of the men, the lucky soul must go through an intense interrogation by the woman, reminiscent of the kind that takes place in Guantanamo Bay. The woman carries out a thorough financial analysis of the male, also taking into account any future prospects. Within two minutes of conversation she has placed him in one of several categories.

1. Loser.
2. Has enough money to buy drinks for me and my friends for the evening.
3. Meal ticket, plenty of money, need to keep him away from my friends.

Men that fall into category one are quickly dismissed. Those that fall into the second category are bled dry up to their credit limits with plenty of Vodka or Champagne ordered for the lady and friends.

The meal ticket, the true objective of every Gold Digger, is an elusive and valuable subject, whom the women will do almost anything for and to in order to achieve their ultimate ambition: a life of ease and luxury at the expense of a man.

# JULY 2ND

What a nice start to the day, an email war with Lucy. Prior to that, things started well with me being woken up by the classic song Waltzing Matilda, not the watered-down, commercially accessible, wishy-washy version sang by Rod Stewart but the Tom Waits original in all of its tortured, lacerated, wretched beauty.

After my flame war with Lucy, I decided to treat myself by wearing one of my favorite outfits, a beautifully cut, tailor-made grey-brown three-piece suit. A good suit should make its wearer feel like a God and those that see the suit want to genuflect and not look in the eyes of the wearer for fear of being turned into a pile of salt. Wore a matching stunning three-button shirt from Circle of Gentlemen without a tie, and turned heads all the way to the bus stop.

Suitably cheered up I arrived in the office where, after an hour and half of waiting, listened to the latest excuse for being late from our departmental secretary Justine, who is really wasted working in the administrative field. I feel that there is a career for her in the TV or movie business, writing complex, thrilling, original plots as each excuse from her is more elaborate than the last and everything is so implausible that, even though I know better, I am almost convinced that there must be some truth in there somewhere. I inherited Justine, a borderline alcoholic English girl, who like cheap German red wine doesn't travel nor age particularly well.

Apparently years ago (she's worked for us for over 10 years) she was a complete looker; well, now she just looks kind of worn-out, like the fruit I sometimes buy from the local supermarket that goes wrinkled and soggy after two or three days. She constantly wears a facial expression that looks as if she's just drank a glass of sour milk. Black hair badly dyed blonde. Huge natural boobs (sadly I must admit having sampled them once after or during a drunken Christmas party) and a sagging stomach to match. The result of years of excessive alcohol use, drugs, unhealthy food and too much exercise on her back.

Justine is smart enough to know that if she were in the UK she would have been fired years ago, but is well protected by Dutch employment law, which makes it incredibly difficult and expensive to terminate employees' contracts. Thus she clings onto her job, like a Gold Digger to a footballer, doing just enough to remain employed and I certainly don't want to reward her financially for her years of incompetence. The fact that she's also suspected of having had numerous flings with various married Partners also makes Senior Management nervous about getting rid of her, in case their extra curricular activities see the light of day. I give her the most tedious tasks possible to deal with in the hope that she'll quit in disgust, but how do you demotivate someone with no ambition beyond getting drunk and high in her spare time?

George slithered into my office.

"Simon, I've got some great ideas on how to improve the way things run in our network support area."

"George, you've only been here five minutes, why not wait till you understand how things hang together a bit better? Once you've done that I'm sure that Remko who is after all your line manager, will be happy to receive some well-thought through input."

"Oh well, if it's like that then I'll make sure to let Remko know." said George in a wounded-weasel-like voice.

"I do think we have some opportunities to improve things."

"Yes, well, as I said talk to Remko, he knows you've got a lot of experience and I'm sure he'll be willing to listen."

"Don't get me wrong, boss, I'm not casting aspersions on your group. You're doing a great job."

"Really? Am I doing a great job? Well, thanks for that vote of confidence George, I'll sleep a lot better at night knowing that you think so highly of my performance." His face went red at this.

Rising to my feet and walking towards the door I said, "Thanks for the time, George, catch-up with Remko when you're ready."

I then briskly exited my office, heading for the coffee machine.

Had a conference call with Christian, my New York based German boss. On Mondays we have the leadership team meeting which runs for 90 minutes, 85 of which are spent with us listening to him drone on like an angry wasp stuck in a glass. He's lived in the US for five years yet still speaks with an accent that sounds like a Brit impersonating a German.

"Wat V have to do is reduce costs and be Agile Ja? I will not be hearing of too much work for ze teams, V must werk harder."

We then had five minutes for 12 people to ask questions, an incredibly productive meeting.

Had a call with members of my Mumbai based "off-shore" team. A cynic might suggest substituting "off-shore" for cheap labor but of course I wouldn't dream of suggesting such a thing. Global organizations must remain competitive, and if everyone is using cheap labor then so should we.

These calls are always frustrating due to heavily Indian-accented English spoken with incredibly creative and liberal use of English grammar. Thus instead of degraded performance we have "There has been a degradation of system performance."

"Do you mean that the performance has degraded?"

"YES, THAT'S WHAT I SAID A DEGREDATION OF PERFORMANCE. ARE YOU NOT LISTENING CORRECTLY?"

With our off-shore team it's certainly a case of their crap, but they're cheap. Twenty cheap off-shore Indians cost the same as two good full-time employees.

"What V have to do is reduce costs and be agile Ja?"

They deliver pretty sub-standard work, make lots of mistakes but ultimately they are so cheap that activities which would have gotten a Western world-based employee fired several times over are excused and accepted as the cost of doing business. I'm being a hypocrite about outsourcing, of course, as when I felt the corporate wind blowing in the direction of India I couldn't jump on the bandwagon fast enough. When saner colleagues were making eloquent arguments for keeping certain activities in-house I took the opposite position and pushed the benefits of concentrating on the core competencies of our organization and the need to remain nimble and flexible, which outsourcing would allow us. This was looked on favorably by the Partners and helped me get promoted to my current position, but, unlike the man that built a house on quicksand and had no intention of living in it, I've actually ended up owning and running the house and spend much of my time trying to prevent nature from taking its course and preventing it from inevitably collapsing in on itself.

Tried to find out the status of my planned business trip that week to Paris, which involved me going on a hunt for Justine, my semi-useless departmental secretary who of course was in our café gossiping with Myra and Bromwyn, two other female colleagues who seem to not be able to get through a single day without spending large amount of times discussing other people's private lives.

I always name the three of them together GNN, the Gossip News Network, as the majority of rumours (founded or unfounded) tend to originate from these three. Indeed, in the past I've found it to be to my advantage that the best way to get information distributed throughout the organization is pull Justine to one side, tell her that something is completely confidential and not to be discussed with anyone. It will then quickly spread throughout the organization. During the height of the credit crisis, when we needed to make a few people redundant, I specifically told her the names of several people who we were considering letting go; within a couple of months they had found other jobs, thus saving McCulloch thousands in redundancy payments.

"Justine, sorry to interrupt your coffee break but have you made the arrangements I requested for Paris yet? It's just that my psychic powers aren't what they were, and having not received any response to my request I just wondered if I have train tickets and a hotel booked for the night."

Flushing redder than a member of the communist party, she gazed upon me with a face that reminded me of a creased and battered mango I saw on sale in my local supermarket once.

"Have a bit of patience, Simon, you've got me doing lots of different things, I can't do everything at once you know."

"*Everything* I know you can't do, but it would be nice if you could just do *something*. I don't see what's so difficult about booking a simple trip to Paris. It would have taken me no time at all to arrange it myself; I'm not asking you to remap the human genome, just book the trip please."

She responded with a stuttering and unsteady voice.

"Yeah well, I had erm… started on it but..."

"I don't want to hear it, Justine, please spare me another epic story of struggle, survival and success against the odds, just get it done please."

Sniffing now, were those tears in her eyes?

"I'll do it right away, I'll drop everything else you and the other team members have asked me to do and I'll tell them that Simon has got to have his Paris trip info."

As I walked away I could hear the clucking of the other members of the Gossip News Network and a hushed "You shouldn't let him talk to you like that."

Thus, leaving the three witches of Macbeth together to plot their wicked schemes, off I went, with a smile on my face.

# THE BALLAD OF PHILOMENA

There once was an English rose named Philomena who didn't take drugs and rarely touched alcohol. She was the first member of her family to attend University, not just any run-of-the-mill establishment but Oxford. She graduated with a First Class degree in Computer Science and had a successful career in IT. Being the industrious young lady that she was, she decided to become self-employed and work as a freelance IT Consultant. She was offered a highly paid six-month contract as a SAP specialist at McCulloch in Amsterdam. Her parents were concerned about her moving to a city that had a reputation for liberal attitudes towards narcotics and sex, but Philomena was a good girl who didn't drink or take drugs.

Upon settling in Amsterdam, being a single lady on her own she worked diligently and gained the respect of her peers as an extremely professional, hardworking and reliable colleague. Socially, however, boredom soon set in. As a single lady living alone in a foreign country, she rarely ventured out and spent most of her evenings at home. To help relieve the monotony, she bought two cats that she named Winston and Clement.

Justine, the departmental secretary, searching for more gossip for her news network, was amazed to find out that Philomena, despite having by then been in Amsterdam for several weeks, had barely been out, apart from some basic sightseeing. Thus like an orphaned kitten she was adopted by the cattiest women known to man: Justine, Myra and Bromwyn. Myra was the leader of the group, an über-aggressive project manager with a talent for stabbing colleagues in the back to cover her own short comings, and Bromwyn, a woman with no visible talents at all apart from the ability to consume large amounts of food several times a day. Philomena was flattered and happy to have something to do other than sit in her apartment with Winston and Clement and gratefully accepted the invitation from the girls to go out for a drink with them.

They arrived at the Three Sisters pub in the RembrandtPlein and the girls automatically ordered some non-descript semi-toxic white wine for her. Not wanting to offend her newfound friends, she gratefully accepted and drank her first glass of alcohol since the previous Christmas, which was about the only time of year that she normally drank. When they ordered another glass followed by several more, being the polite and good-mannered lady that she was, she followed suit and drank each glass she was offered.

There once was an English rose named Philomena who didn't take drugs and rarely touched alcohol and whose two cats were called Winston and Clement. For the next few weeks this became a regular occurrence. She would go out with the girls and end up drinking several glasses of wine or more. She often staggered up the winding stairs to her apartment in the Kerkstraat and had to carefully hold on to the banister on the way up. Also unusually for Philomena, who was previously renowned for her punctuality, she often found herself sleeping through the alarm and arriving for work late and slightly red faced, with a headache that often lasted into the afternoon.

Justine also introduced Philomena to her favorite pub, the Whisky Bar in the Korte Leidsedwarsstraat. It's there that she also began sampling different types of whisky on a regular basis. She found that she had a real love for single malt whisky and, for the evenings when she had to work late from home and couldn't go out and join the girls (all of whom were single), bought herself a bottle of whisky to keep at home in case she fancied a glass or two while working.

Even though she had little or nothing in common with Justine, Myra and Bromwyn (apart from their land of origin), it could be said that the four became firm friends and of Philomena, whereas it was no longer the case that she didn't drink, she at least didn't take drugs. This was of course soon to change.

There once was an English Rose named Philomena who didn't take drugs and rarely touched alcohol and whose two cats were called Winston and Clement. As she was spending more and more time out of the house, the cats (who were lonely and frustrated) would urinate and defecate all over the apartment, something that she was often too inebriated to deal with when she got home. She would wake up in the morning to the smell of stale urine, or step on cat faeces in the bathroom, which would set her incandescent with rage. The cats sensing this would run and hide to avoid the wrath of their mistress.

One day at work while Philomena was in the ladies' toilet, she heard giggling and whispering from the next cubicle. Recognizing Justine's voice, she tapped on the door and asked to be let in. Justine and Myra were together and she couldn't help noticing that there were traces of white powder on Justine's face and nose.

"What are you two doing?"

"Is that what I think it is?" asked a clearly surprised but curious Philomena.

Myra responded: "Yes, it is what you think it is, but you're too much of a goody-two-shoes for it."

Philomena who previously didn't drink or take drugs, denied being a goody-two-shoes and asked if she could try some of what the girls had.

"Are you sure?" asked a surprised Myra.

"I don't think this is you really," said Justine in an enquiring tone.

Philomena took the folded 20 Euro note that Justine had quickly closed in her hand and proceeded to sniff the white substance that was neatly laid out on a hand mirror. Sneezing and gasping, she felt a sudden rush of exhilaration and hot flushes all over her body.

"You all right?" asked a concerned Justine.

"The first time is always amazing, but not easy."

"I'm not sure how I feel actually, not really sure if I feel anything at all," replied Philomena, who previously didn't drink or take drugs.

Later that afternoon, Philomena had a feeling of unlimited possibilities, she felt powerful, omnipotent, invincible almost. At a meeting to discuss a plan how to implement a new version of SAP, her newly-found confidence brimmed over, leading to several surprised colleagues being shouted down by her when they didn't agree with her ideas on how to move forward. Several people in attendance at the meeting gave each other sideward glances and the meeting drew to a close without having the main topics discussed due to Philomena's insistence of arguing every point raised that didn't agree with hers.

Following the meeting she was called in to speak with Tim, her manager, an American Expat that had lived in Amsterdam for over 12 years and still couldn't speak a word of Dutch.

"Is everything ok with you? Are you having problems at home?"

"No everything is fine with me, why do you ask?" replied a surprised and mildly irritated Philomena.

"Well, it's just that we've noticed changes in the way you work and I have had to comment several times about your time keeping lately as well, and I don't know quite how to put this but well, you ought to think about paying some more attention to hygiene matters."

She felt herself flush hot and trying to control her voice

replied: "I beg your pardon, how dare you comment about my hygiene, what's wrong with it?"

Tim shifted uncomfortably in his seat and trying to keep his voice steady said:

"There have been some complaints about you coming in the morning smelling of alcohol. I remember what it was like when I first moved here - I went wild, partied, drank, did other things as well. What you do in your spare time is your business, but don't let it interfere with your work, we pay through the nose for your services and want you 100% sober and alert, ok?"

That evening she met up with Justine for a drink and asked her if she had any more of the drug she'd taken earlier, pointing out that she was happy to pay for more.

"Pay?" said Justine in a shocked voice.

"Only idiots pay for it, come with me, I know where we can get some free."

The pair jumped into a taxi, which smelled as if the owner had been cooking garlic on the seats. After directing the driver the entire way, they ended up in the Bijlmer area of Amsterdam, outside a building made of concrete, where loud music could be heard blaring from within and lots of people hovered around outside.

"Are you sure it's safe here?" asked a visibly nervous Philomena.

"Ooh listen to Lady Muck. Sorry, love, if the neighborhood isn't upmarket enough for you. Don't worry though, no white girls have had anything happen to them here that they didn't want," said Justine with a secretive smirk on her face.

"Of course it's safe, we're cool, I know people here."

They took a lift up to the fourth floor of the concrete monstrosity with the music and commotion getting ever louder. They entered the second apartment on a long balcony full of apartments. As soon as they walked into the apartment, the strong smell of marijuana filled Philomena's nostrils. She'd tried some as a student and had never understood people's attraction to it.

In the street where she lived in Amsterdam there were several coffeeshops and a low cost hostel across the road. She often smelled marijuana and was used to seeing stoned and drunk tourists staggering around at all hours.

They entered a small apartment which was packed to the rafters with people who couldn't have been older than in their mid-twenties, dressed in running shoes, track suits and Lycra.

Justine introduced Philomena to a man of Indian- looking complexion who must have been at least 190 cm tall. Justine whispered something to him and he broke out into an infectious smile and greeted Philomena with a huge bear hug. He called out something in Dutch to one of the track-suited youths who were sitting on a worn-out sofa, smoking what looked like a large homemade cigarette.

"This is my friend, she's new here, and you must look after her."

"Don't worry; I'll treat her like a princess. What your name again babe?"

"Philomena, without the babe."

"Oooh, we got a fiery one here, I've just the thing for a fiery hot woman."

He disappeared and returned with a glass containing some unspecific-looking liquid and gave it to Philomena who not wanting to be rude nervously gulped it down.

"What's this that I'm drinking?"

"Firewater honey, for a woman of fire."

"Firewater? What is it? It tastes like Schnapps mixed with Prosecco."

"What the problem?" asked the Giant in reply.

"Justine drinks it like it's water. Look, she's on her second glass already."

Philomena hadn't noticed, and had a warm glow from the drink. Not wanting to be rude she accepted a refill as the Giant poured more into her glass.

"There, that's more like it, there's a good girl. Don't worry, there's plenty more where that come from."

Justine looked at the Giant and putting on a little girl's voice said, "As we are being such good girls, can you share some of the stuff you have with us?"

"If you two keep on being good girls, I'll be happy to share with you, but you two need to share with me," he said mysteriously.

Another glass of firewater was poured into Philomena's glass. There once was an English Rose named Philomena who didn't take drugs and rarely touched alcohol and whose two cats were called Winston and Clement.

The next morning at 11, Philomena was awoken in her bed by the sound of her Blackberry ringing. Her head felt as it had been used as a punch bag and she slowly crawled out of bed. She noticed that her thighs ached, as did many muscles throughout her body. She also had a burning sensation in her nostrils. She couldn't remember how she got home.

As she made her way to the bathroom, she was shocked to see that the door was closed and heard the sound of the toilet flushing. As the door opened, the Giant from the previous evening greeted her standing naked with an "Alright babe? How you feeling? You got through some serious amount of weed and coke last night, and the way you drunk down the firewater, wow. You know, they say that English girls are nasty in bed? Well damn baby, now I know why they say that, you are one nasty bitch."

As she listened to this shameful scenes from the previous night came back to her in flashes. Sniffing lines of white powder together with Justine from his chest. Playing drinking games with him and Justine. Passing an ice cube from her mouth to his and then on to Justine's. He and Justine both were kissing her breasts at the same time. His huge penis in her mouth, inside her (did he use a condom?) - Oh God, what had she done? Her swallowing his sperm (something she never did normally, she was a good girl), her head spinning and Justine's tongue licking her and she holding her head down and sucking the guy while Justine licked her!

She stormed pass him into the bathroom where she vomited loudly for several minutes.

After throwing the man whose name she couldn't even remember out of the apartment, she called in sick to work, then went back to bed to sleep off her hangover and the shame she felt for losing control. Upon waking up eight hours later, while getting dressed and going into her handbag she found a sachet of white powder and some pre-made rollups that could only contain marijuana.

She decided that a single joint wouldn't do any harm and followed this up with several glasses of whisky from the bottle she'd bought previously.

There once was an English Rose named Philomena who didn't take drugs and rarely touched alcohol. Over the next few weeks her attendance became steadily worse. In spite of the shame she felt of her wild night with a complete stranger, once the white powder she found in her bag ran out, she called him and began seeing him on a regular basis, usually ending up with him fucking her brains out in return for supplying the drugs she now took on a daily basis. Being of a generous nature he also started sharing the delights of Philomena with a good friend of his. She initially resisted but was so desperate for another line of coke that she did what his friend wanted. The first of many "friends" whom she would have to entertain.

Her colleagues filed several complaints about her increasingly unkempt appearance and unpleasant smell. She also became emotional, unpredictable and difficult, if not impossible to work with until the management team at McCulloch decided they had no choice but to terminate her contract. Her close friends, the Gossip News Network, distanced themselves from her as quickly as they could, however continued to provide regular updates to her former colleagues on Philomena's ever deteriorating state.

The last I'd heard of her was that one night she came home in a drunken stupor and put her two cats, Winston and Clement, into a box and then took them to the Prinsengracht canal where she threw the box into the water. Fortunately for the two cats, a small boat was moored underneath where she had thrown it, so the box and the cats were found. Due to the cats having been electronically tagged, the police were able to trace Philomena as the owner. She was arrested and fined for animal cruelty and neglect.

# JULY 3RD OR GENTLEMEN'S CULTURAL EVENING

Finally after a long and miserable winter we're experiencing a hot summer in the Netherlands! Is there anything better than being in Amsterdam during hot weather? Lovely long-legged ladies (who would normally be badly dressed) wearing so little that I have to spare my usual fashion criticisms. I took a shower and a shake consisting of low-fat yoghurt, Brinta (look it up), blackberries, blueberries and raspberries quickly blended in my space-age KitchenAid Artisan blender. A metallic beauty, sensual to the touch that looks so good in my kitchen, I could weep. I put on a three-piece mohair navy blue suit with white piping. Matched this with a pink Circle of Gentlemen shirt and a pair of Brogues from Church's shoes, which are made for Gentlemen but they still allow me to buy them. I looked so good that my reflection almost shook my hand. I smelled good as well. I resisted the urge to have a quick game on the PlayStation or to look at any quality German porn and headed out to my waiting driver.

One of the things to be recommended about Amsterdam is that women see no problem hopping on a bike and cycling while wearing a mini skirt. Short shorts are all the rage at the moment as well. So got into my private Uber taxi and travelled along to work with a smile on my face.

In the Netherlands the powers that be wisely deregulated the taxi business. This led to a free-for-all with many dishonest semi-criminals from all over the country descending on Amsterdam with the aim of making a quick buck. Getting a taxi became a gamble and an expensive activity, as aggressive taxi drivers would demand outrageous amounts of money for driving short distances. "You want to travel 2 kilometers? That's 25 Euros."

I lost count of the number of arguments I had with aggressive taxi drivers trying to rip me off. Luckily I read about a private service that has fixed prices and drivers who are not only polite but don't complain when you want to drive shorter distances. I've never looked back since using them and refuse to take normal cabs any more if I can help it. The only use S Class Mercedes, BMW 7 series, larger Audis and Jaguars. That's how I roll. Had a pleasant, air-conditioned journey to the office.

Had the usual day at work, spent justifying the existence of my department (or justifying the unjustifiable), as it's budget planning time. The grandson of one of our firm's founders (Miller) is now Chairman. A job that I'm sure he has got only through sheer hard work and talent. His being related to the founder has, of course, nothing to do with it. Since taking over the Chairmanship six months ago, he's had the management team running around like headless chickens organizing an operational efficiency review. If carried out properly the results should be interesting as by and large we are incredibly inefficient. This is masked by charging our clients exorbitant amounts of money for delivering common sense solutions wrapped up in hundreds of pages of PowerPoint slides and strategy documents.

So spent most of the day on Excel and PowerPoint before leaving the office with my token Dutch friend Koen and with Richard. Koen, like myself, is a lover of fine dining and had booked a table at the latest "in" hotspot in Amsterdam, the newly opened Oyster Kings in Amsterdam South.

First impressions were pretty good. The place had recently been renovated and was a mix of soft lighting, marble, chrome, and glass. We were welcomed by a leggy, lovely-looking black lady whose head was full of teeth so white they could light up a dark room. She was slim and had the kind of body you'd want to eat your dinner off. Richard, a lover of black women, broke into a huge smile as he saw her and whispered, "If the women in here look like her, I'll be a happy man."

As she showed us to our table, I looked around the room and could see groups of (shock) well-dressed women in their thirties and forties. Lots of designer stiletto shoes, bags from Louis Vuitton, Michael Kors and stylish sexy clothes that were actually colour-coordinated. Also a few tables of guys like Richard, Koen and myself, obviously having business dinners. Obligatory iPhones and Samsung smartphones on display and probably a few Blackberries hidden away out of embarrassment.

Upon being seated and setting our iPhones on the table, we had an in-depth intellectual discussion about the quality of the ladies in the restaurant.

Richard: "I don't fancy yours much," he said looking at a thirty or forty-something woman who'd obviously made too much of the recent weather and was wrinkled like an old prune.

"I'm shocked at how many well-dressed ladies there are in here," I commented.

"It's as if I've walked through a portal and have ended up in Paris, Munich or any other city but not Amsterdam. Look at the ladies on the table over there: sexy shoes, outfits, well made-up. I'm in window-shopping Heaven."

Koen asked with an exasperated tone, "Why are you so

obsessed with how the ladies dress? It's when they're naked that matters, not what they dress in."

"That's the typical response I'd expect from a Dutchman," I replied. "The packaging is just as important as the package. If you buy an Armani outfit they don't just throw it in an old wrinkled plastic bag."

Having agreed to disagree on which ladies were the finest, we realized that we'd been sat at the table for fifteen minutes already and had yet to be offered a drink or a menu. Koen caught the attention of a waitress who appeared to be too busy talking with a colleague to serve our table. She didn't look amused at being interrupted in her discussion on world peace and the pros and cons of nuclear fission.

We ordered three glasses of Champagne as an aperitif. Whenever I'm asked the question "Would you like an aperitif?" I always want to say "Why, what's wrong with my own teeth?"

The menu looked pretty good, with a wide range of seafood and fish on offer. I decided to go for the three types of fish tartar, as did Koen. Richard likes his food to be in the manner of so many female TV presenters in the UK, dull, simple and predictable, with as little flair as possible.

Upon reviewing the menu he looked in disgust at the two of us and said, "If you expect me to eat this muck, you've got another thing coming."

A surprised Koen asked, "What do you mean by muck?"

"Come on, the menu looks great."

"Great? What's great about fucking oysters and seafood?"

"You knew we were going to a fish restaurant, or did the name Oyster Kings lead you to believe we were going to an Argentinian steak house?" I asked while shaking my head in disbelief at his complaining.

"Oysters are eaten by ponces, poofs and toffs," responded a red-faced Richard whose voice was slowly getting a little too loud.

"Thank you, Professor Richard, for that insightful view, no doubt based on vast amounts of research. Why don't you calm down and select something from the menu that you can eat?" suggested Koen. "There's also steak on the menu and Surf 'n' Turf."

"Listen guys, I just hate the poncification of good old-fashioned food, but at least there's something on the menu I can eat. I'll take the Surf 'n' Turf. Half a lobster and some steak will do the trick for me." I also ordered the same thing and Koen ordered the Tuna Steak on a bed of Spaghetti.

Naturally the waitress didn't bring us a wine list and after waiting another ten minutes one finally arrived. A boy who looked as if he should still be at school nervously took our wine order of Pouilly Fume. He looked incredibly stressed when I requested this so Koen repeated the order in Dutch. The stressed boy with sweat on his forehead and a look of terror in his eyes asked Koen to point out the exact place in the Wine list where the wine we wanted could be found and looked relieved after he also spelt out the name phonetically. This left me with an impending sense of doom about the rest of the meal.

Several glasses of wine later, (the bottle delivered by the shaking boy who almost dropped the bottle and cooler on the floor) the starter of three types of tartar arrived. It looked as if a trainee who had just started working in the kitchen against their will put it together under duress on the same day. The presentation was terrible, and one could only conclude that it was a form of rebellion from the person enslaved in the kitchen. Three flavourless types of tartar were gone in three bites.

Richard, who'd skipped the starter, commented, "If the main course is not much bigger than the starter, it will be a trip to McDonald's later."

The waitress returned to our table and with a blank stare and a tone of voice that sounded as if her question was well rehearsed asked, "Did you all enjoy the starters?" "Are you genuinely interested? Or is this just something you're supposed to ask?" I put this to her with eyebrows raised. "Well of course I'm interested, that's why I asked," she replied. "Ok, as you were kind enough to show an interest, I'll give you an honest answer that I hope represents everyone seated here. The starter had no flavour and reminded me of the title of a well-known film, 'Gone in 60 Seconds'. It had the taste of Lady Gaga and the Kardashians rolled into one, in other words it was completely tasteless." The waitress, still staring blankly at us, replied: "Oh that's very nice to hear, thank you."

We ordered our second bottle of wine and the main course arrived. The tuna steak on a bed of Spaghetti ordered by Koen was floating in water.

"The spaghetti needs a diving suit, the poor tuna is going to drown in that much water," said a laughing Richard.

The biggest surprise though was saved for the alleged half a lobster that looked as if it had suffered from a serious bout of anorexia.

"Half a fucking lobster? Half? I'm no mathematical genius but if that's a half, I'm an Amsterdam taxi driver who knows where the fuck he's going and doesn't drive the long way round or fiddle with the meter to rip-off tourists," shouted an enraged Richard.

The waitress came over and I said to her, "The opinion of this table is that the half a lobster comes either from an escapee from an Anorexia clinic for Lobsters, or never grew up to become an adult lobster and we are eating the remains of some poor lobster child that, like Oliver Twist, spent its days in some workhouse squealing in a wounded voice: 'Please sir, can I have some more?'"

"That's how we serve it," replied the unmoved waitress.

"In the words of a tennis player that you're probably too young to remember, a Mr. John McEnroe: 'Oh come on, you cannot be serious?' That lobster had an eating disorder, how could it have been so thin?" I asked incredulously.

"I'll get the manager," replied the now red-faced and extremely pissed-off looking waitress. After what seemed like an age, along came a woman in her twenties, the alleged manageress.

"I understand that you have a problem with your food?" she asked the table.

Richard, by now extremely agitated, replied: "Listen, love, the tuna, if it was still alive, would drown in the amount of water that's come with the spaghetti, and that's saying something for a fish. If that's half a lobster, then I'm the next King of the Netherlands."

Looking at Richard, Koen and I as if we were something stuck to the bottom of one of her rather cheap-looking shoes, she responded in an equally loud voice as Richard by saying, "Many famous people eat here and have never complained as much as you three have tonight."

Not quite believing my ears, I looked at her and said, "I don't base how good the food in a restaurant is on how many celebrities eat there. This is the Netherlands after all, how many famous people do you have in the entire country? Surely all three of them can't eat here? The menu says quite clearly half a lobster, not half an escapee from an eating disorder clinic. For the prices you guys are charging I would have expected a bit more food and lot less bad attitude from the staff. Just remember that the year is 2013 and the Internet is not your friend. We'll be posting our opinion of your establishment on multiple sites. The motto of your business is obviously 'Never mind the quality, feel the width.'"

"We won't be coming here again; we'll leave plenty of space so your famous customers can enjoy it even more. We'll have the bill now, please."

When it did arrive we paid 100 Euros a head for a substandard meal and were still hungry on leaving.

Suitably disgusted, but merry from the wine, Richard suggested, "How about a visit to the Red Light District?"

Well, it would have been rude to say no, therefore, putting the needs of a friend ahead of our own, we accompanied him to the area of Amsterdam known only too well by British tourists, foreign businessmen and the hardest working ladies in the country, wandering along a road of well-lit windows full of women in underwear advertising their wares like a stallholder in a marketplace, a meat market. As we wandered along, Koen suddenly stopped and stared at one window in particular where a woman who did look vaguely familiar swore at us and then drew the curtains closed.

"Oh, my God," I said to the guys, "wasn't that Philomena? "Fill-a-whom?" asked Richard. "An ex-colleague of ours," Koen replied.

"Unbelievable! I'd heard rumors, but my God! Well, if you know her, knock on the window and see if she'll give me a discount, she wasn't bad looking," commented an extremely sensitive Richard.

"You've got to be kidding," I said incredulously, "she looks rough, and do you really want to have it off with someone who's had God knows how many men in a single day?"

"You're too posh for me, Woolcot, nothing wrong with sloppy seconds as long as you wear a diving suit. Who said the English were Gentlemen?" said a laughing Koen. "Well, Richard, if you want to sample the services of Philomena, go ahead. We're off to see a live sex show."

"Oh come on, I was only joking. If you're going to a live sex show you'll need the assistance of an expert in such matters; I'm in."

Live sex shows are one of the "cultural" activities that many tourists come to Amsterdam to see. The people who run Amsterdam City Council are desperate to play down the importance of the Red Light District and of the Coffee shops selling not coffee but various types of Marijuana. Instead, the new puritans are desperate to promote Museums and Art

Galleries. As if Berlin, Paris, London and Prague don't have all these things already. In how many places in Western Europe can you legally have sex with a prostitute, go and smoke a joint afterward, then round up the evening by going to see people having sex on stage? The reality is that many tourists come to Amsterdam and do all of the above, including visiting Museums.

There are at least two live sex places that I'm aware of in Amsterdam. Being the classy gentlemen we are, we chose the Teufel, which is one of Amsterdam's oldest of such establishments. For a Wednesday evening the place was packed. It resembles a theater, with over 180 seats and a stage in the middle. As we were queuing to buy tickets, we were behind a group of giggling American (or Canadian; who can tell the difference?) girls and a mixed group of guys and girls from somewhere in the North of England. Having paid the reassuringly expensive entrance price (40 Euros!) we made our way upstairs.

Paid another outrageous amount for a round of beer (yes I have been known to drink it occasionally) and took some seats next to a mixture of semi-drunk, horny, curious, seedy, cheering and leering fellow audience members. Loud Euro-pop music was blaring so loud that we had to shout above the noise to be heard. The lights suddenly dimmed, the deafening muzak lowered and on-stage the curtains opened to reveal a revolving love-heart shaped bed. On the bed were seated a fit-looking guy in his thirties in boxer shorts and a woman in cheap-looking lingerie who possessed what we gentleman would describe as a butter face. Nice body but-her face!

The audience of misfits all began cheering and shouting as one as an old song from Color Me Bad – "I Want To Sex You Up" came on loud as a plane at take off. The woman on stage romantically pulled down the guy's boxer shorts and started pulling in a monotonous and vigor fashion on his semi-erect penis. Loud female cheers and screams from behind where we were sitting almost deafened me. Various comments in multiple languages were shouted out. Whether they were insults or encouraging comments was difficult to ascertain.

After pulling on the guy's cock as if she were changing the gears on an old manual car, the lady (of whom I'm sure her parents were proud) stripped out of her underwear that was so cheap even refugees would have refused it. She then took his now fully hardened member in her mouth and began sucking on it in a fashion which led me to believe she wasn't particularly excited. After only a few sucks, the guy bent her over and slid into her from behind. They then began having sex in a pretty mundane fashion to the cheers of the overexcited crowd. In front of me in the next row a couple obviously aroused by the action on-stage practically began putting on a show themselves in the seats. The amateurs were almost better than the 'professionals' on the stage, which revolved slowly to ensure that all of the patrons in the theater didn't miss out on any action.

On it went, two not particularly attractive people having what looked like the sex I imagine goes on between couples that have been together for years. The ability to surprise and excite has gone, only to be replaced by a well-rehearsed routine.

"Nice job," shouted Richard, a little too loudly.

"Hope they're paying him enough to shag that thing."

"Keep your voice down you idiot, do you want us thrown out of here?" I hissed urgently at him.

"What? I paid 40 Euros to watch a bloke porking a kitchen nightmare with as much excitement as if he's taking the rubbish out. I've got a right to comment."

"What do you mean kitchen nightmare?" I asked.

"Did I say kitchen? She'd be a nightmare in any room of the house, especially the bedroom."

At precisely this point, the only other person in the establishment apart from ourselves who was wearing a suit made his way over to us. He looked as if he ate whole cows for breakfast and lifted cars for exercise. He was at least 190 cm tall and probably half as wide. In a strong Dutch accent and in a polite but threatening tone, he proceeded to say, "If your friend doesn't keep his mouth closed for the rest of the show, all three of you will have to leave."

A chill of terror ran through my bones. Richard, once he's had a few drinks, tends to believe that he is the last representative of freedom, democracy, and all that is good in the world. A nervous-looking Koen hissed at Richard: "Shut the fuck up, don't say another word."

This is where things really began to go downhill. Richard turned to the giant and fearlessly, some would say stupidly or even recklessly, shouted, "Sorry big guy, but I thought Holland supported freedom of speech, which is a democratic right for all residents of Holland."

"You may be right," replied the giant, "but you are not in Holland, right now you are in my private island. I'm the prime minister, president, King, Emperor and Queen and I've just passed a law that says drunken idiots must be deported."

As he said this, Koen and I jumped to our feet and (being the brave and fearless men that we both are) apologized on Richard's behalf.

"We're sorry, we don't want any trouble, we'll get off your island right now."

By now the curtains had closed and the crowd was hurling insults at us.

"Throw them out, fucking losers."

Richard, now angrier than ever, shouted:

"Who you calling a loser? Fuck the lot of you, why are you here? To get tips for the bedroom cause your own sex life is so fucking boring. Bunch of limp-dicked, Sahara desert-dry-pussy bitches and wankers."

"That's enough," said the giant threateningly.

"You can't throw me out, I've got rights." As he said this, Koen and I had both noticed several fellow giants coming up the aisles of the theatre from all directions.

"Richard, we're leaving right now!"

"Listen to your friends, short boy," said the first giant with a tone that would have scared Special Forces soldiers.

"Richard, we're out of here."

Moving with as much dignity as we could muster, and trying not to run, Koen and I made it out of the theater in one piece. I'd recently spent a fortune on orthodontic work to correct years of British dentistry and wasn't in the mood to have to repeat the exercise. Shaken and definitely stirred, Koen and I parted ways and I jumped into a taxi home.

# HOW TO DATE DUTCH MEN

I recently had to go to the Marriott Hotel to collect a colleague who was visiting from the US, Dave Goodman, and take him to our office in Amstelveen. He was supposed to be meeting me in the reception area but wasn't there when I arrived. I asked the receptionist, a lovely Russian lady, to call his room but there was no answer, so she made an announcement over the PA system. "Paging Dave Goodman, can you please come to reception? Calling Mr Goodman." She tried this several times and then in exasperation she said to me: "Wow, a Goodman really is hard to find."

This brings me to the topic of today's blog post. Think of Ahab's quest for Moby Dick, John Ford chasing the elephant, Wile E Coyote's hopeless pursuit of the Road Runner or Tom's obsessive and hazardous campaign to capture Jerry. Since the dawn of time, man has risked life and limb to hunt down its prey.

The lovely Jasmina, Olga and Niamh Ni Bhroin have reached out to their Uncle Shallow Man for advice on how to capture that most exclusive, reclusive and elusive of prey, the Dutch male. My advice may be controversial, however, like Brian who was crucified on the cross for his beliefs, or that great leader of the Roman slave rebellion of old, I will stand up, unafraid and shout out: "I am Spartacus" without fear of the consequences. The things I do for my readers.

Every man is different, so of course I will have to generalise. The tips I will provide are just ways of helping to (at least) get as far as a good conversation, or, better still, the things that Expat women should not say to Dutch men.

## Religion

To get anywhere with a Dutch man you have to be able to understand, respect and tolerate their primary religion which is money. Dutch men worship money above just about anything else.

When going on a first date with a Dutchman, the Shallow Man's first piece of advice is to not react in shock, disgust or reach for the sunglasses if, as is highly probable, he turns up wearing a pair of bright red jeans. This is considered by many Dutch men to be the height of chic and elegance. Indeed, I suggest to compliment him on his bold and daring use of primary colors and try not to stare at them for the rest of the evening.

Due to their love of money, you should not be insulted at the end of a delightful evening at some nondescript brown café, when your date goes through the bill with the scrutiny of an American customs agent checking baggage for the presence of illegal substances. The Dutchman's love of money will make him check every item on the bill several times and then, with the speed of a supercomputer, calculate precisely how much your portion of the bill will be.

"You had the white wine, that's 5 Euros, we had bitterballen to start, there were 6 but you had 4, which means that you need to pay 2.37."

If you wish to get into a Dutchman's heart, you need to accept that there are three of you in the relationship: him, you, and his money, which he will cling onto like a Gold Digger to a footballer.

When he presents you with your portion of the bill, smile gracefully and pay your share as if this is the most normal thing in the world.

### Common Mistakes Made By Expat Women When Hunting Their Dutch Prey

When chasing their prey, a common mistake made by Expat women is to dress well. In other words, not wearing jeans or old boots that look as if they've been handed down from mother to daughter to granddaughter. Expat women have also been known to visit hairdressers more than twice a year and they are also not strangers to wearing make-up. This can make the skittish and highly sensitive Dutchman extremely nervous. A well-dressed woman with styled hair and make-up might be after the thing he values most, his money.

To stand a chance with a Dutchman, my advice is to take a flight to London. Find a homeless person that fits your size, and then pay them some money to hand over their jeans, which should be in a pretty poor state. Wear the jeans, along with a pair of second-hand boots purchased from Marktplaats (the Dutch ebay) and for the rest of the outfit follow the example of Dutch women.

Turn all the lights out in your apartment then reach for the first thing that comes out of the wardrobe. It will definitely not match the rest of the outfit. Take a salad strainer or colander, put this over your head and then turn on the tap for 30 seconds. Leave your hair wet then put on a heavy metal song and shake your head in time to the selected track for another three minutes. This will make your hair fit the style typically worn by Dutch women thus naturally attractive to Dutch men. Do not apply any make-up.

### Hairstyles Of Dutch Men

The Netherlands is an incredibly flat country, thus it can be extremely windy here. The most common form of hairstyle for the Dutch male is one that is aerodynamic and reacts well to the windy conditions of this country. Dutch men typically have their hair combed backwards in the style of the Lion King. My advice is not to be surprised that most men have this hairstyle. Don't hum the tune to "The Lion Sleeps Tonight" while running your hands through his hair.

### Fashion

Dutchmen and brown shoes go together like drones and dead civilians, Amsterdam and high apartment rental costs, Miley Cyrus and bad taste. I guarantee that on your first date with a Dutchmen the standard uniform of brown shoes, blue jeans, a smart shirt and a suit jacket will be worn. This is because like their female counterparts, Dutch men believe firmly in "Doe Maar Normaal," i.e. do not under any circumstances display any individuality in case you stand out.

### Equality And Dutch Men

If you do manage to bag yourself a Dutchman and end up moving in with him, you'll be the witness to an incredible transformation. The once proud Dutch lion will become a pussycat. Dutch women, even though they typically only contribute less than 25% of income to the household firmly rule the roost and wear the trousers at home. Visit any V&D or major store on a Saturday and you'll witness the once proud Dutch lion being bossed around by his poorly dressed partner. Once you have a Dutchman he will expect you to bark orders at him like a circus trainer shouting at his animals. Don't forget this as otherwise he'll be unsettled in the relationship and may go elsewhere for a bit of tough love.

## Flirting And Romance

The female friends of the Shallow Man inform me that your expectations in this regard should be lower than a snake's belly. Flirting typically involves a coffee, some bitterballen (which, as I stated above, you'll be expected to pay 50% of), then a quick invite back to his cave for a night of horizontal jogging.

# JULY 4$^{TH}$ OR THE LAST CHAMPAGNE IN PARIS

Awoken at 5.50 am by a What'sApp message from Irina.

"I horny and want to suck cock"

My head still pounding from the combination of too much wine and excitement of the previous evening and taking into consideration that I needed to catch a train to Paris at 8 am, I thought it over for 1 millisecond and replied:

"Come round to my place right now you hot whore"

Obviously, I hoped that it was **my** cock she wanted to suck.

Twenty minutes later, in walked Irina, wearing a full-length leather coat that ran almost down to her Stiletto boot-covered feet. Without saying a word she stepped out of her coat to reveal a bodice, stockings and suspenders. She went straight to her knees and good to her word licked, kissed and sucked my cock as if it were her last meal on earth. She was so wet, my fingers slid into her like an Olympic Skier down a slope. I took my soaking wet fingers out of her, which we both licked, then kissed each other to savor the taste of her sex. I slid my fingers into her again and proceeded to feel her dripping pussy until she stopped me and breathlessly said: "I don't want cum yet, fuck me now."

Being so turned on we didn't even go to the bedroom but had a frenzied fuck right there on my living room floor for the next forty minutes. Breathing heavily and covered in sweat we had a passionate kiss and then I told her that she really needed to be going as I had a train to catch to Paris.

"You love the home delivery fuck, no? I went to bed horny thinking of you and woke up so wet, I had to have you," said a smiling Irina still licking her lips from the beautiful mouth in which I'd recently deposited a vast amount of sperm.

"Forget fast food, I prefer a fast fuck any day. You're incredible! I've never had a woman text me like this and just come round to fuck."

"Really? Good to know. I also have certain urges, needs, passions. You are convenient for me as I am to you."

Ah, the romance.

She then kindly joined me in the shower, bending over so I could quickly enter her. I hung on to her beautiful breasts for dear life as we fucked once more. Have you ever fucked in a shower? Awkward, slippery but, by God, exciting!

Having dispatched Irina, I hurriedly got ready, even skipping the spreadsheet and choosing my Scabal, Prince of Wales checked bespoke three-piece suit to wear with a Canali yellow silk tie and a Circle of Gentlemen white double-cuffed shirt. I looked in the mirror and my reflection wanted to shake my hand, as I was so damn good-looking.

Even though I'd only be staying for one-night I packed an additional suit, a two-piece chrome blue beauty, with a light blue Pakkend shirt to match. Packed my Armani boxer shorts and Burlington socks, plenty of condoms, then hopped into my waiting Uber with Irina's taste still in my mouth.

Caught the Thalys train to Paris just in time. Sitting in 1st class, I devoured the breakfast served there, sharing the details of a croissant that might have seen better days with my followers on Twitter. During the 3 hour, 14 minute journey, tried to put thoughts of my vigorous session with Irina out of my mind and focus on the purpose of my two day trip, a final meeting with a new supplier who'd be providing us with a new Datacenter facility for our French operations.

As much as I love having an excuse to visit Paris, this meeting was completely unnecessary. Following months of negotiations, the contracts have actually been signed. The tasks in hand could easily have been conducted via Tele/ Videoconferences/email. There was no urgency for this meeting. However, my manager, Christian, felt it was so important to have this meeting that he'd flown in from New York to attend. I checked into my Hotel, Le Meridian Etoile then took the subway to La Defense for the meeting at our Paris offices.

The meeting was scheduled to start at 2 pm and I was due to have a pre-meeting briefing with Christian and the team at 1 pm. Along with him from our New York office came Bernadette, a thirty-something, slim, muscular-looking Jamaican from our supplier management department. She was so tough that rumor had it she spent her spare time walking into bars in the Bronx, daring people to fight her. She had the eyes of a serial killer and a Medusa-like stare that could if not turn people into stone, at least make them feel stone-cold.

My German Fraeulein Anna was also in attendance, having flown into Paris earlier in the morning. Unusually for a German she hated trains and would fly everywhere, even when (as is the case with the Amsterdam-to-Paris link) the train would be more convenient.

Looking at his watch, Christian, who is about my height, 180 cm but at least 10 to 15 kilograms heavier, gave me a warm greeting.

"Simon, so typical of you that in a meeting with two Germans, a Jamaican and an Englishman you are late."

"Well Christian, lateness is really a matter of perspective. The meeting in my calendar says 1 pm, however as I'm so well prepared for this meeting, I didn't think it was necessary to attend for the first 15 minutes thus allowing me to check into my hotel. Always remember that to look this good does require extra time."

"I'm not finding that funny, Simon, can we get on with the meeting?"

The intended purpose was to go over our operating agreement with the supplier. Christian was dressed smarter than usual, in an off-the-peg two-piece pinstripe suit which he'd unwisely kept buttoned up while sitting down. This gave the impression that his stomach was a prisoner, desperate to push its way out of the jacket. For some reason he'd chosen to wear a checked shirt and polka dot tie with the suit, which made him look like someone auditioning to be a clown at a circus.

The real purpose of the meeting was for Christian to attempt to impress the Account Director of our new supplier, the lovely Claudine. The rest of us were there to demonstrate how powerful Christian was and what lowly, clock punching cogs in the corporate wheel we were, compared to this fine specimen of business leadership.

At 2 pm on the dot, her punctuality obviously part of the appeal to Christian, in wafted the lovely Claudine on a cloud of exotic-smelling perfume. She brought along two colleagues, Nadine and Daniela. Claudine stood at least 185 cm tall in her Louboutin shoes, with long brunette hair, skin that looked as if she bathed in Yaks milk and a finely tailored business dress that subtly hinted at what were probably magnificent breasts desperate to shout out "Here we are, world, we dare you to look."

The business suit was made of some fine material and clung to her Heavenly curves like a newborn baby to the nipple. Christian rose heavily from his chair, straightened his suit and greeted her with a hearty "bonjour, Claudine' followed by a kiss on both cheeks. She returned his greeting with the kind of French accent that I often fantasized about (ok, masturbated over) during my early teenage years. Age-wise, Claudine could have been anything from 25 to 50. It was impossible to tell and given the looks that she's been endowed with, who cares.

Christian (was he starting to perspire slightly?) turned and said, "Claudine, dis iz **my** team: Bernadette, who I believe you have spoken to before Ja? Anna from Legal, I know you already met." With a slightly lower tone in his voice: "Simon Woolcot, who is very difficult to forget."

Claudine introduced us to Nadine, a French, mousey- looking blonde in her early thirties who looked like she could do with eating a decent meal or three. She was underweight. I was concerned that if she walked alone through a field a bird might mistake her for a twig and carry her off to use as material for a nest.

Daniela was a hard-faced-looking Croatian. I'm sure she laughed at least once or twice a year, probably in winter when old age pensioners fall over on ice and break their hips. She was from the Suppliers Service Management team and a counterpart to the equally tough Bernadette. If I had to put odds on the winner of a fight between the two I'd wager that East European viciousness would outweigh Jamaican ferocity.

For the next three hours Anna, Bernadette and I listened to the Gospel according to Christian.

"Wat v must do is…"

"U agree with me Ja?" asked Christian over and over again like someone suffering from Tourette's syndrome cursed to shout out the same phrase ad nauseam.

The lovely Claudine's voice rose and fell like a raft on a wave, while Christian droned on in a relentless monotone that had my mind wondering. Scenes of Irina's legs spread wide underneath me floated before my eyes. Her juices on my tongue, my cock in her mouth.

"Simon, I asked you about our delivery service level agreement."

"Err, what? SLA? Right, sorry I was a bit distracted. Where were we?"

"Perhaps it's time for a coffee break Ja?"

"U agree with me Ja?"

As we separated and I came out of the men's toilet I bumped into Daniela, the hard-faced Croatian.

"You were really distracted no?" she asked in an almost friendly tone, for her.

"I'm sorry if I caused you to lose your concentration. I know what the looks you were giving me mean, you bad, bad boy."

"Errr, I think there might be a little misunderstanding here."

"No misunderstanding, don't be embarrassing, you are a man, I'm an attractive woman, of course you stare at me. Funny, men normally want Claudine; you, Simon as I know by the way you dress have a good taste. We are going to dinner together this evening, we drink something after, ok?"

This was said in tones that were more of a threat than a promise.

Hell on a bicycle! The hard-faced cow thinks I have the hots for her. As John Wayne said in the Searchers, "That'll be the day."

How do I get myself into these situations? Thanks, Irina. Back at the meeting I did my best not to stare at Daniela for the rest of the afternoon, which was difficult considering she was sat opposite me. I know now how a turkey must feel just before Thanksgiving Day, as she sized me up with the cold and precise calculating stare of a poultry farmer.

Following the meeting we headed for dinner at L'Avenue, a chic restaurant near the Champs-Elysées with deep red velvet décor over two floors. It's one of the Paris "in" places. I once had the misfortune of being seated close to Kanye West and Kim Kardashian. The place caters for the rich, famous and those with generous expense accounts. All of the waitresses are part-time models dressed in killer heels and designer outfits, oh and the food, almost forgot to mention the food which is pretty good, but people don't really go there for the food. Because beautiful women staff the place, and as I said earlier, I can forgive a beautiful woman almost anything, I suggested the venue as the place for our business meal.

Of course the lovely Claudine not only knew the place but also was a regular.

"Oh Simon, what a good choice of restaurant," she said in her singsong accent while lightly touching my arm for just a little too long.

Christian, not wanting to be upstaged by an underling and wanting to also impress Claudine, said, "Vis is a good restaurant, I know it well, but next time, we will go to the restaurant of the Hotel Costes, and it's much better than this place."

"Actually, Christian, the Costes Brothers, owners of the Hotel Costes, also own L'Avenue. This has the exact same menu as Hotel Costes," Claudine pointed out in her beautiful accent.

"Really? Well I vink that Hotel Costes is better."

A vision in a frilly pleated short skirt and heels so high that if she fell she'd have needed a parachute, tottered over to our table and took our drink order. Anna leaned over to me and whispered in German: "Put your eyes back in your head, you might need them later. I know now why you chose this place."

Bernadette and Daniela spoke to each other, making awkward forced small talk, while Christian bored the rest of the table with his knowledge of fine wine, Paris, Outsourcing, World Politics, Economics, Indian Food Recipes, Beer Gardens, the best places in New York you've never heard of and the ever changing price of pork. Claudine, Nadine, Daniela, Bernadette and Anna smiled and laughed in all of the right places of his story and listened attentively to his never-ending monologues.

Nadine of course didn't order a starter, lest she should consume more than the 500-calorie a day diet she appeared to be on. I was sat in between Anna and Daniela, whose left leg would press against mine from time to time while making tedious conversation with Christian. I should say, while trying to make conversation with Christian, who doesn't believe in pauses during conversation.

After a glass of champagne and several glasses of Pauillac my mind was strong but my body was weak. The surreptitious rubbing of Daniela's leg against mine had stirred my cock to life and evil thoughts were going through my head. Anna, Bernadette and Christian (the suckers) were staying at a Hotel in La Defense, whereas mine was in the Center of Paris. After we left the restaurant, following Christian making a big deal of charging the meal to his Corporate American Express, Christian, Bernadette and Anna said their goodbyes and jumped into a Taxi heading to La Defense.

My Hotel wasn't far from the restaurant.

"Well, ladies, it's been a great evening and as my Hotel isn't far from here I'll walk back."

"No, no, Simon, you cannot go back to the Hotel yet, the night is still young," said a smiling Claudine. "You're from the UK, are you not? I thought you guys like to drink?"

"Well, Claudine, if you have a suggestion, I don't mind going somewhere else for a drink. Do you have anywhere in mind?"

Nadine, who barely ate anything during the meal, announced she was tired and would head home, leaving me alone with Claudine and Daniela.

# HOW TO MAKE FRIENDS WITH THE DUTCH

Many older former people of faith eventually come crawling back like husbands that have had a brief affair with a younger woman, humbled, to their religion. One of the reasons for this is the fear of certain death and eternal damnation, which brings me to the subject of this post.

Many Expats look up to me as a kind of land-bound, better-dressed version of Christopher Columbus, and have asked for my advice on navigating the choppy and uncharted waters of relations with the Dutch. With tears on their keyboards, they have written to me and asked "Shallow Man, we've lived here for years and still have no Dutch friends, why is it so difficult to get to know them on a personal level?"

Indeed, many Expats live here in the Netherlands in a kind of social Purgatory, trapped between Heaven and Hell. They can see all of Dutch daily life going on around them, but are not quite involved due to lack of any meaningful friendships with the locals.

Being the selfless person that I am, yet again I will step into the intercultural breach and this time provide advice on how to befriend the Dutch and reach that desired state of integration Heaven - having a Dutch friend. This will no doubt be controversial in some quarters, and yet like Miley Cyrus at the VMA awards I will twerk my perfectly formed bottom at my critics, even if it means being locked in a room by angry Dutch people and forced to listen to Andre Hazes' greatest hits while watching TV shows featuring Linda De Mol. The things I do for my readers!

Over the years, the Shallow Man has wandered through the Dutch wilderness, from Hoorn to Harderwijk, Den Bosch to Zwolle, from Utrecht to Maastricht, and from the Bijlmer to Rotterdam Zuid and has gathered much experience in dealing with our denim-clad, brown-shoe- wearing hosts. Following my wandering in the wilderness, I have returned with advice on how to become friends with the Dutch.

## Thou Shalt Have No Other Gods Before Me

A common question asked by Dutch people is "What do you think of Holland compared to your own Hell-hole–of-a -country-that-is–not-the-Netherlands?" A character trait I admire in the Dutch is the willingness not to allow a complete and utter lack of facts get in the way of a good lecture of the pros and cons of a country they have never lived in. When asked this question always reply how much you love this country compared to your own and how much better the quality of life is here; that will immediately score you some despite-being-a-bloody–foreigner-knows-his–or-her-place brownie points.

### Doe Effe Normaal

As I've posted elsewhere, being smartly dressed, for example wearing black shoes, heels, make-up, not wearing denim and taking care of one's appearance is generally frowned upon. If you dress in a way that is outside the "Normen en Waarden" (i.e. Norms and Values) of Dutch society, you will be labeled as someone who thinks too highly of themselves. If you want to get on, dress as if you are going to pick up some plants from the local garden center. This will make you less suspicious to the locals who will relax and might even involve you in a conversation.

### The Language Death Spiral

Here is an interesting conundrum. If you speak Dutch with a local, the response you'll receive will invariably be in English. However if you speak in English you'll be asked "How comes you don't speak Dutch?" Breaking this vicious cycle without causing offence will require the delicate diplomatic skills of a UN negotiator. If your Dutch is good enough then politely insist on speaking Dutch as you wish to improve your skills. I've known fluent Dutch speakers who've lived and worked here for years that still get spoken to in English by the locals.

Be persistent and even if they respond in English, continue speaking Dutch. This should hopefully wear them down and have them speaking with you in their language. The effort you make in speaking Dutch should with most reasonable people play in your favour.

For the "How comes you don't speak Dutch?" question, don't get defensive. Simply reply that you've tried to learn the language but found it too difficult. This will often go down well and give them a warm feeling of superiority and a chance to show off their English skills. Do not under any circumstances tell the truth which is that as hardly any countries of global economic importance speak Dutch and since you only plan to stay here for a couple of years, it's not worth your while to bother learning it.

**Transparency**

In most countries in the world the invention commonly known as curtains is still widely used. Here in the Netherlands, with its open society, such things are not regarded as necessary. To befriend the locals, it won't help if you make sarcastic jokes about looking through people's windows and watching them eat Frikandel while counting their money due to the lack of curtains. When in conversation with the locals compliment them on the financial astuteness of not having to waste money on unnecessary dry cleaning.

**Why Expats Can't Make Friends With The Dutch Two Views.**

**View 1**

If you work in one of the larger cities in the Netherlands, such as Amsterdam or The Hague, you'll find that most Dutch colleagues who have children will live well outside the city, in small towns where house prices are cheaper. As much bonding and friendship often starts with drinks after work, this often excludes local Dutch colleagues who have to rush off home to their demanding partners or to collect children from childcare. What then transpires is that the only people who tend to socialize regularly outside work are the Expats who often, at least to begin with, are on their own.

**View 2**

As Dutch people, they already have a circle of (local) friends and don't want to expand their circle with Expats. The view is often: " Why should I make new friends when I have them already?" Some might say that's a selfish, anti-social and narrow-minded point of view but it's certainly one I've heard mentioned by Dutch colleagues over the years.

**Enter the Circle of Death**

If you do somehow manage to overcome all of the obstacles mentioned above you will not only become friends with a Dutch person, but also end up being invited to attend a "Party." Many cultures have their own ideas of what constitutes a party, but may have never experienced what those of us in-the-know describe as the Circle of Death. This is a slightly surreal experience. A group of Dutch people will sit together in a circle. Alcohol is often not served. Hapjes (tiny hors d'oeuvre), small bites of bitterballen, cubes of cheese and that exotic delicacy - crisps in a bowl - are provided.

The gathering then sit together and talk, with much use of the word "Gezellig" coming into play. It's an interesting experience to say the least. If you experience this, then you've arrived and have a genuine Dutch friend.

## Summary

There's an old saying that I firmly believe in: "I would never want to join a club that doesn't want me as a member." This is particularly true when it comes to making friends, regardless of the nationality. There has been a nationalistic movement in this country that started with Rita Verdonk (anyone remember her?) and has continued with Geert Wilders.

The doctrine spouted by these people is that foreigners who live here should want to be Dutch, in other words resistance is futile and assimilation is the only option. It was a strange mentality believing that when you move to another country, you should strip away your national identity, want to be something else and become a cardboard cut out Dutch person that doesn't really exist. This may seem strange, because integration does not mean assimilation.

Thankfully such views are held by a relatively small (I hope) subset of people in the Netherlands. By and large, I've found the Dutch to be pretty open-minded, fair and friendly people. It is difficult to make friends with them and I would say that they are actually less open than for example the Germans and even the French, but that's just my personal experience.

People should accept you for who you are. If they don't want to be friends with me because I'm not from some small village in the Netherlands, so be it. I've made some good friendships with Dutch people and we've bridged the language gap without much of a problem. Keep an open and positive mind and only good things can come of it. This is a wonderful country and I'm happy to be here, and to people who can't appreciate the value of a friendship with someone as they are not from the Netherlands I say: Hou right Op!

# JULY 5$^{TH}$ OR MANIC FRIDAY

The world was dark, bleak, and desolate. I was in a strange bed, God knows where. In the distance I could hear a trumpet playing, then a gravelly voice, then of course Louis Armstrong's "La Vie en Rose". My head felt as if it had been put in a vice and squeezed just before the point of crushing my skull. My tongue was drier than the feet of a camel. Then there was a strange smell in my nostrils, the pungent smell of Claudine's perfume! I turned slowly, ever so slowly in a king size bed and realized that I was at my hotel, alone. What the fuck? Only one thing to do, postpone the alarm and go back to sleep.

My iPhone ringing. Shit, it's Christian, it's 9 o'clock, and I should be in the office. I answer the phone.

"Simon, have you mastered the art of invisibility?"

"Sorry? The art of what? I've no idea what you mean," I moaned into the phone in a tortured voice.

"I am speaking with you, yet you are not in the room with me so I assume that you are:

A: Undurchsichtbar (invisible).

B: Not here and late for our meeting.

It seems that you are not the only one who is unpunctual. Neither Claudine nor Daniela is here either. Would you know why dat iz?"

"I'm not a mind reader, so can only speak for myself. I've overslept and will be in the office in the next 45 minutes."

I fell out of bed, laid on the floor. Crawled across the room in the direction of the bathroom and felt as if I had two obese women on my back. Once I made it there I proceeded to throw up into the toilet so loudly that someone knocked on the door and asked if I was all right. Once there was nothing left to repeat (something I wish many television companies suffered from) I stood under a freezing cold shower, and screamed like a little girl. Brushed my teeth for at least ten minutes, gargled with huge amounts of mouthwash. Even the use of my lotions, after shave and dressing in my chrome blue suit for once didn't leave me with the feeling that I looked good. In fact I looked as if someone had danced on my head and felt as if the Dutch national football team had taken turns in kicking me around a field.

I staggered into a taxi and arrived at the office shaken, stirred, and sick as a dog that had found out its new master was from Korea. Upon arriving at the office I drank enough coffee to affect its price on the commodities market, then finally faced my boss and colleagues.

"Good afternoon, Simon," said Bernadette in a triumphant voice. She's never liked me and now she had something on me that she could score points with, what a bitch.

"I find it irresponsible that you are so late, yet again!" cried Christian in a voice of doom for my career.

"Christian, unless you'd like to nail me to a cross right now I suggest that we move on and have the meeting."

"How can we have a meeting? Only Nadine is here. Where are Claudine and Daniela? Did you take them somewhere after dinner?" He asked eyeing me suspiciously, his voice rising at the same time.

Claudine walked in, smelling and looking wonderful. Upon seeing and smelling her, Christian's entire demeanor changed instantly. It was like St Paul's story, the scales fell away from his eyes and suddenly the world was a different place.

"Claudine, how are you on dis beautiful morning? You are looking very gut."

Indeed, even through my hazy state I could see that she looked very good. A blind man could have seen it. She was wearing a matching cream skirt and lacy top that clung on to her breasts for protection. Cream-colored high heeled shoes and probably matching cream underwear, if she was wearing any at all.

Oh how my poor head, my body, my very soul all hurt.

"Where is Daniela? asked Bernadette, in a both aggressive an suspicious tone.

"Oh, Daniela called me early this morning; she had an urgent personal matter that she must attend to. She sends her apologies, but, Christian" she said touching his arm, "I'm sure that **together** we can work through everything that we had planned today."

Was I being paranoid or was she deliberately avoiding eye contact with me? I was too ill to care. My poor head, my body, my mind, my soul, my ancestors, and the kids and the grand children that I might have in the future were all in pain. The universe hated me and I hated it back three times as much.

"Simon, tell me who did this to you and I will have them killed," said Anna to me later in the morning. "You look as if you are about to slip away from this world into the next. You have eyes that are almost closed, skin that looks not right and a voice that sounds like Marlon Brando in the Godfather." She was definitely laughing at me and not with me.

"Anna, I'm dying. Avenge my weary corpse."

"What happened to you?"

"I don't know." I whined like a wounded dog. I was trying to be a man and not burst into tears or throw up.

"The Dutch have a saying, Simon: 'Be a man during the evening and a man in the morning.'"

With such tender sympathetic words I returned to the meeting and tried to remain alive. I've never thrown up during a meeting before but, good God, I came close to decorating the meeting room table and Claudine's fine cream outfit with liters of vomit.

I was never so happy to see the Thalys pulling into Gare du Nord to take me back to Amsterdam. Needless to say I slept all the way back home and had to be awoken several times by a guard who didn't believe that my shambolic, hung-over self should have been in first class.

# JULY 6$^{TH}$ OR EXPAT PARTY

Date: July 5th 11.39pm
From RichardC2000@Outlook.com
To:Simonwoolcot, KoenV@McCulloch.com

Subject: Some mates you are

Oi, you bastards. You left me on my own at the sex club to face down those… ANIMALS. My democratic right to free speech was threatened. Not just mine, but yours as well. "Tyranny reigns when good men do nothing", Jean Luc Picard, Star Trek the Next Generation. He was fucking spot on. You bastards were out of that club quicker than a banker out of a brothel. You bastards call yourself friends? Disgraceful behavior. From the Dutch I'd expect no more, but from a fellow countryman? Woolcot, you're a traitor.

For the first time in many a year I stayed in on a Friday night. Did you know that if you buy milk and leave it in the fridge too long it turns into a smelly gunk? Upon opening the fridge on the return to the Woolcot palace and smelling the stale milk I had another bout of throwing up. Stomach finally settled, I did the only thing I could do which was to walk down to my local Thai place, Thai Deum on the Ceintuurbaan and get a takeaway rice dish.

Caught up with Game of Thrones, or I should say that I tried to, but fell asleep within about 10 minutes. Woke up on the sofa at 1 am, crawled into bed.

My dreams were disturbed. Flashes of Claudine touching my arm; I could hear Daniela's voice but it sounded different. It was stern, soft, insistent, pleading. Loud music played in the background, lots of faces, beautiful people. Claudine's perfume, my hotel bed, my phone ringing in the background, messaging and a fierce-looking guy with Claudine.

I awoke with a startle, breathing heavily. Looked at my iPhone that was on the drawer next to the bed. 10.15am. I missed a call from Irina. She'd also sent me some What's App messages.

11 o'clock on Friday evening: "Where u at darling? You back in Amsterdam? Shall I come to you and sit on your cock?"

Two o'clock in the morning: "Why you no answer? I'm wet for you, come and fuck me or are your still in Paris? I can join you if you wish."

Finally started feeling like a human being again. Had a long soothing bath, followed by smothering myself in Vichy body lotion. Had a shave, used some Chanel face cream, Chanel Egoiste aftershave (what else?) after which I dressed in my full Armani outfit. A combination of Armani boxer shorts, black jeans, an Armani T-shirt, belt and a super thin silky-to-the-touch Armani leather jacket. Also wore a pair of reassuringly pricey John Richmond sneakers. Feeling like a male supermodel that's just been put on the cover of GQ, I strode or should say strutted out of the Woolcot palace with confidence to face Amsterdam on a Saturday.

I live very close to Amsterdam's allegedly famous street market, the Albert Cuyp. I'd never heard of it before moving here, but hordes of clueless tourists in the neighboring streets almost walking in front of cars, bikes and trams while looking for the market on their smartphones are proof of its fame throughout the world. I strolled along the Ferdinand Bolstraat then turned onto the Albert Cuyp Straat, where I decided to take a walk prior to going to Café Binnen en Buiten, where I'd arranged to meet a pissed-off Richard for breakfast.

The sun was shining and the streets were packed. The pent-up fury, tension, and aggression of Saturday shoppers was in the air. Throngs of people swarmed through the narrow streets of the Albert Cuyp Straat like ants over a discarded half eaten apple. People with bags, with children, with friends, lovers, mistresses. People with baggage, both emotional and shopping, people with yappy little annoying dogs, digital cameras, pit bulls, smartphones, people flirting, joking and making passes, folks with saggy arses. Bankers squeezing past off-duty tram drivers, plain-clothes police looking out for thieves. Shifty-looking Romanians scanning the area for easy prey, stallholders seeing what semi-rotting fruit they could sell today. Giggling teenage girls, boys pretending to be tough, British Expats feeling unusually rough. Ladies old and young eating raw herring, a peculiar-looking man suggestively squeezing a mango with a leering smile, two men kissing while a disgusted-looking light brown-tinted guy looked on. The hunger-invoking smell of roasting chicken, Turkish food, pancakes, Belgian fries and freshly roasted nuts. The smell of raw fish, the familiar noise of people shouting into their smartphones, smatterings of conversation, parents telling kids to hurry up, the crush of hundreds of people squeezing through the narrow street. Perception overload and there's nowhere in the world I'd rather be on this sunny Saturday morning.

I wandered through the market, then headed towards the Ruysdaelkade to meet Richard at Café Binnen and Buiten. The Ruysdaelkade is an odd street of the kind that you can only find in Amsterdam. It's partly residential but also between the junction with the Ceintuurbaan and the junction with the Albert Cuypstraat there is a mini Red Light District. Two or three floors of windows occupied by an assortment of multi-colored women of the world provide services of the bedroom kind 24 hours a day, all year round. The red light windows are closed off at either ends of the street by an assortment of bars and a swanky upmarket Asian fusion restaurant.

Gathered near the windows full of scantily-clad working ladies, like animals around some African watering hole, were a group of guys shouting, laughing and sneaking glances at the ladies. A couple of women parked their bikes on the street in front of the windows, while embarrassed-looking men exiting the rooms held their heads down to avoid the knowing gaze of the women and scurried away like cockroaches disturbed by a suddenly switched-on light. Never walk past the windows on a hot day; the rancid smell of stale sex fills the air. I also never walk past there at night, as, just like nearby watering holes after dark, the animals get restless.

As Richard saw me approaching the Café where he sat outside drinking a coffee, he theatrically pointed at his watch. The terrace outside the Café was packed with posh braying students, estate agents with bad haircuts, jeans and brown shoes. Lots of women talking so loudly, that I could pick up fragments of conversation:

"She said something terrible about me on Facebook. He sent me a picture of his nipples on What'sApp. We were at Jimmy Woo and took some photos that we posted on Twitter." The usual deep conversations held by the Internet generation.

After listening to Richard having a go at me for being late as usual, I sat down and ordered an Uitsmijter, a combination of fried eggs, bacon, cheese and bread. Good post-hangover food. Richard had decided not to wait for me and was already tearing his way through a chicken sandwich as if it was the first time he'd eaten in a week. He was wearing grey trousers, a thin woolen jumper that had holes from where the moths had been at it and a tweed jacket on the shoulders of which copious amounts of dandruff sat. Looking at me with a touch of contempt and with a mouth full of food he told me the sorry tale of what happened after Koen and I made our strategic retreat from the live sex show.

Richard: "After you two ran away like the poofs you are, I looked at the first bouncer and said, "listen mate, you're messing with the wrong guy, here, just cause you're a big bastard doesn't mean I can't drop you like a sack of shit.". The giant looked at me and started laughing then reached to grab my arm, I blocked it and then did a Jason Bourne style combination on him, blow to balls, neck and chest in lightning-quick time and he dropped quicker than the knickers of a Polish woman on a first date. The audience stood up and started cheering. The second bouncer, who was also approaching from the other side, just stood there shocked. I shouted, "You want some? Come on then, you fucker", but he started backing away. I then gave the giant who was on the floor rolling in agony another kick and then legged it out of there."

I listened carefully to his story and said, "Nice, so what really happened?"

Opening both hands in a pleading fashion, Richard replied, "What? You don't believe me? God's honest truth, that's exactly how it went down."

In a weary tone I said to him, "So you want me to believe that you suddenly developed unheard-of unarmed combat skills to take down a giant and scare the shit out of the giant's big brother as well? This is your third and final opportunity to tell the truth, don't waste it."

Breathing a deep sigh he pointed at me and (in an accusing tone) whined, "Well, I blame you and Koen for what happened. If you'd backed me up, then things would have been different. As you and Koen ran out of the sex show, the first giant reached out to grab my arm, so I did the only thing that a man in my situation could do."

Intrigued now, I leaned forward and asked, "Which was? What did you do?"

Richard, blushing slightly, "I made a deal with the devil."

Somewhat confused, I asked him, "You did what?"

Lowering his voice, an irritated Richard responded, "Are you deaf as well as a coward, Woolcot? I made a deal with the devil. I'm not a religious man, well, we both used to be… remember, all those years ago at Mary and Michael's…?"

"Don't remind me," I responded. I'd known Richard for many, many years. We were at the same primary school as kids in East London, where men are men, and the sheep are afraid.

Being two years older than me, Richard had gone on to secondary school then we'd both gone on to study at the same University and as is the way of the world, it was Richard that had originally introduced me to a Partner at McCulloch and had helped me get my first job on graduating University. He'd later joined the Amsterdam office, not long after me. We'd long before turned our backs on the Catholic indoctrination, bullying and brainwashing that we'd received both at home from our parents and from the primary and secondary schools we'd attended, which made it all the more unusual to hear him speaking in such biblical terms.

Looking at him with some concern, I asked, "So the devil works at a live sex show in Amsterdam, does he? Tell me more."

Looking exceedingly shifty, even for him, he proceeded to explain that the giant of a bouncer had grabbed him and was forcibly dragging him out of the club when Richard (fearful of receiving a beating) had turned to him and said, "Listen, if you do me a favor and let me leave here uninjured I could be of some value to your club".

I tried pressing him on how on earth a 165 cm IT guy could be of any use to a live sex club, but he refused to divulge any more details.

"Let's just say that, as I said, I made a deal with devil." "What kind of deal?" I asked. "The kind of deal that let me keep my legs and allows me to get back into the club any time I like free of charge." He said this while looking into his first beer of the day and not so subtly avoiding eye contact with me. "Don't worry mate, I won't be performing on the stage if that's what you're worried about," he added, somewhat optimistically.

I burst into hysterical fits of laughter, causing the posh students and estate agents, all desperately trying to appear to be cool, to turn in our direction. Shouting loudly is acceptable on the terrace of Amsterdam cafés, but laughing is frowned upon. When I recovered from my laughing fit, I decided to give up trying to get the information out of him on what kind of deal he'd managed to close with the sex club bouncer, at least for the time being. A big mistake that I still regret to this day. Had I pushed him, what later happened to my old friend could have been prevented.

Richard warned me to stay well clear of his brown sugar, the formidable Marcie, a 178 cm tall, 95 kg heavy bruiser from Surinam who (he informed me) would like to kick my skinny arse up and down the Albert Cuyp Market. She'd have to catch me first and I can run bloody fast when I have to. Apparently she blamed me for the live sex show fiasco, and was unjustly under the impression that whenever something negative happened to Richard, I was always nearby. With the threat of confronting the formidable Marcie in the air, we said our goodbyes and realizing that I might need to sprint away from Marcie on sight, I changed into my running gear and did a swift 5 km run along the Amstel River and back home.

Having showered, applied the appropriate amounts of grooming material and dressed in my Armani combo, I decided some late afternoon aerobics with Irina were called for. As I arrived at her pokey apartment and rang the doorbell, there was no answer. Strange, as I could see that her light was on from the street. I tried a couple of times then, thinking that she might be in the shower, also tried calling her as well but to no avail. Somewhat deflated I headed frustrated back to the Woolcot palace.

That evening an Expat event was planned. There's a complete market in Amsterdam of various clubs, which organize social events aimed at Expats - something of which Amsterdam has plenty of. Meetup, Internations, Meetin, there are plenty of groups out there looking to take the Expat Euros and the Expats have plenty of Euros to give away. Saturday evening's event was arranged by Expatnation, a group specializing in arranging events for upmarket Expats, meaning anyone who can afford the 45 Euros a month membership fee. The seemingly extortionate membership dues are more than justified by the fact that each event is packed full of hot and generally available women, many of whom are new or alone in Amsterdam. The members of Expatnation tend to be slightly older, thirties to fifties and generally in fairly senior roles within large organizations. This is to be both a curse and a blessing, as the allure of lots of Expats with large amounts of disposable income tends to attract Gold Diggers of both sexes.

I took a long bath (a luxury in Amsterdam, as many apartments don't have them) and following another round of impeccable grooming, shaving, plucking ear and nose hair and having another shave, headed for the walk-in wardrobe. Opted for a pair of black Karl Lagerfeld jeans made of such a fine material that they could pass for very smart trousers. Opted for a Bogosse black shirt with white stitching running in patterns over it like a train tracks through the country; this I matched with a Circle of Gentlemen black blazer with white piping. I also put on a pair of hi-gloss Chelsea boots from Church's. Looking and smelling like a million bucks, no, make that a billion.

I ate dinner at the fabulous Lebanese place called Artist, that is just at the end of my street. I headed home again to brush my teeth, reapply some Chanel face cream then I headed out of the Woolcot palace towards the College Hotel where the evening's Expat party was being held.

I decided to put Irina and the events of the previous day in Paris behind and me and focus on the party to come. My entire body tingled with excitement. Meeting available hot women at the event was as likely as Lady Gaga putting too much of her body on display and making yet another awful single. Marcie had Richard under lock and key for the night, as did the respective partners of Koen and Nathanial. Anna had decided to attend and I was going to meet her there. Meet, meaning say a quick Hello and then stay well away from her in case some hot thing mistakenly believes that we are a couple.

As I strolled along the Roelhof Hartplein towards the hotel I was in such a good mood that I didn't even swear at a dumb bitch with a hairstyle out of the Flintstones and a rotting pair of jeans who nearly hit me by cycling on the pavement while reading her Smartphone. "There's plenty of room on the road, darling," I shouted after her as she weaved her way unsteadily along the pavement, scattering pedestrians like pins in a bowling alley. As I entered the College Hotel, a beautiful marble and chrome 4 star Hotel, I wondered what my old dad would have made of this.

Glenn Woolcot was working class and proud of it. He started out as a bus conductor and spent thirty years on the buses in London, eventually becoming a bus driver and proud union representative of the Aldgate Bus Garage. Glenn loved God, my mum and the union. The list of people and institutions he despised was so long that it would have taken the creation of a Wiki to list them. To keep things simple, he hated most things including his only son, who he felt was a bit of a poof, since I had no or little interest in the following:

- Becoming a footballer
- Driving a bus
- Joining a Union
- Class warfare
- Becoming a priest

He was also a good friend and drinking buddy of Richard's father, another union firebrand, active in the local church and in the pub afterwards. My dad never let the facts get in the way of a good argument. What the Sun said was generally right, which was confusing for me as he was a left wing Labour voter all of his life and yet was happy reading a newspaper that was avid supporter of Margaret Thatcher, the woman he liked to compare with Satan. If he'd seen me walking into a four star hotel dressed like a King, or at least a Prince, he would have flipped. No doubt he was turning in his grave.

I arrived at the bar and lounge which was reserved for the Expat event. I was not so much greeted as snarled at by Liesbett, a 185 cm Dutch blonde whose face was always set in a permanent sneer. She was supposed to be the host for the evening's event but had the kind of demeanor that could only lead one to conclude that the world was about to end in a few minutes and that none of her childhood dreams had been fulfilled. I never quite understood why she bothered to host Expat events when she always wore the kind of expression that looked as if she'd sooner throw her guests to lions rather than be a pleasant host. I assumed that the pay must have been worth the inconvenience of having to deal with a bunch of foreigners, most of whom didn't even speak Dutch.

"Hello, Simon, are you on the guest list?" she asked with a tone that implied she hoped to God I was not. Having thoroughly double-checked the list she gave me a name tag, essential for these gatherings in case one of the Expats gets so drunk that they wake up no longer knowing who they are. I accepted the nametag with a smile and on walking past her into the bar threw it in the nearest bin. The smell of too many types of perfume hit me. I scanned the room to see if there were any strategic targets available.

An interesting mixture of people had already arrived.

Numerous nationalities were crammed into the room. The dress code for the event was summer elegance; I guess that elegance has a different meaning in many languages. I moved panther-like to the bar, acknowledging the lecherous glances of some women with a smile and ignoring the steely looks of jealous men who knew just by looking at me that they were simply not in my league.

I was in a good mood and ordered a glass of Champagne. To my left were a group of Italian guys who always seemed to move together in a pack, like wolves. In spite of the reputation Italians have for high fashion, these guys obviously hadn't read the memo. They were in jeans, trainers and non-descript poor quality clothing. They had circled a tall brunette with breasts that appeared to be attempting a prison break from the confines of her top. She was in a matching black-and-white skirt and top combination with killer heels. She looked none too pleased to be the center of attention of a group of men who acted as if they had just been released from ten years of hard labor in a prison camp.

To my right were a couple of Indian guys chatting politely with a couple of slightly overweight and poorly dressed British girls. I wanted to run over to the Indian guys and say "NOOOO don't do it, don't waste your time with British girls, they are either all, crazy, alcoholics, or will eat you into poverty." Being the polite chap that I am, I left them to it; less competition for me.

I moved away from the bar, past the desperate Italians over to an American guy I knew from these events, Scott. "Hey Woolcot, how's it hanging, big guy?" Why do so many Americans use this phrase? Does he really want to know how my testicles are positioned at any given moment? What's the correct answer to that question? "Well, they are hanging a bit to the left, I'll have to readjust them later to the center." Scott works for a bank (I think) so I asked how things were at the bank. "I work for Shell, not a bank," he replied slightly irritated. "Oh well, banks, oil companies, same thing right? Both have licenses to print money."

He laughed at this and he held up his beer and we toasted to a good night. I caught the gaze of the brunette that was still being asked multiple questions by the pack of hungry Italians. I smiled, walked over, reached out my hand to shake hers and said, "How are you? Long time no see. Scott's here as well," I said pointing towards a confused Scott at the bar. "You remember Scott, right?" She gave me what seemed like a relieved look. "Of course I remember Scott, how could I forget him?," she said smiling at me through a set of perfect teeth and with an accent that was difficult to place but was definitely Eastern European. Result: "Ciao gentlemen, enjoy your evening, I'm sure we speak later."

As she accompanied me to the bar to meet her long lost friend Scott, the Italians began speaking rapidly to each other in their native tongue. "We see you later, be sure," they called after her. The looks of sheer hatred they shot after me didn't bode well for my continued good looks and health and I made a mental note to steer well clear of them now and in the future.

"Thank you so much," she almost whispered in my ear. I smelt a rather off-putting perfume but as I said earlier I can forgive beautiful women almost anything. As if to enrage the

Italians even more, she looped her hand through mine as we walked to the bar. "What is your name, by the way?" she asked. "You've got it in one," I said. "My name is by the way." She threw back her head and made a sound that I recollect from my teenage years when Richard and I used to rent horror films from the local video shop. The crowd at the bar froze, eyeing me suspiciously as if I'd driven a knife through her heart or showed her my penis, both of which would cause a scream.

When the wailing stopped she squeezed my arm so hard that I feared that my PS3 gaming days might be over and shouted, "Oh, you're sooo funny!" What in the name of Bob Marley had I hooked myself up with? The thought went through my head and I immediately decided to work on an exit strategy who fortunately happened to be standing at the bar and whose name was Scott. "Hey, Scott, let me introduce you to…?" "Natasha, my name is Natasha and, seriously, what is your name?" She asked still laughing too hard. "I'm Simon, my friends call me Woolcot, and so you can call me Sir."

"Haaaaaaaaaaargh," she screamed; nearby I heard the sound of glass breaking as (in shock, no doubt) someone had dropped his or her drink. "As I said, this is Scott, he's from a small country called the US and you're from…?", "Russia," she responded, to which my penis immediately hardened.

"From a small country, called the US," she screamed. People nearby glanced inquisitively at us. "You are very funny, like Vladimir Putin." Up until that point I wasn't aware of Comrade Putin's ability for humor, but apparently he often made jokes in his speeches that Natasha thought to be hilarious. Ignoring Scott she began to throw lots of questions at me as if I were a dartboard and her life depended on hitting the target.

"Where you from?"

"London? I love London."

"How long you have been in Amsterdam?"

"You have family here?"

"What you do here? Oh you're a Director? How exciting, how many staff do you have?"

"How old are they?"

"How many direct reports?"

"Where do you live?"

"In the Pijp part of Amsterdam Zuid, I love the Pijp."

"Where do you go for dinner?"

"Which bars you go to?"

"What's your favorite food? You drink champagne? I love

men that drink champagne, I love champagne."

After taking the not so subtle hint I bought her a glass of champagne in the hope that this would at least shut her up. She'd pretty much ignored Scott so far, which concerned me as my exit plan depended on those two getting on. "Scott also lives in the Pijp," I said to her, trying to elicit some interest in Scott. "Really?" she asked, her voice suddenly cold and sounding uninterested.

"So, Simon, do you live alone?" she asked with her voice suddenly rising and regaining way too much emotion for me. "Alone? No, I'm one of life's natural hippies and share my apartment with 20 people from 19 countries, that's just the kind of guy I am." Of course I shouldn't have dared making another joke as she then began roaring like a seal that's about to be clubbed for its skin. At that precise moment my lovely German token female friend, Anna, walked into the bar. I used this opportunity to make a swift exit away from the howling Russian and Scott, passing the Italians at a safe distance and then greeted Anna.

"Save me, Anna, I'm losing my patience and my hearing." She scanned the bar slowly and then asked me which woman I needed saving from. I tried to subtly indicate the brunette at the bar but as I did so Natasha whose gaze I suspect never left me for a second waved and then boldly walked over, introducing herself to Anna.

"I'm Natasha, who are you? she asked Anna briskly. "I'm Anna," she responded, somewhat surprised, "pleased to meet you, Natasha."

"How do you two know each other? Are you work colleagues?" she asked. I looked pleadingly at Anna, hoping she would say something to get me off the hook. "Yes, Simon and I are work colleagues, nothing more in case you're interested."

"Thanks for nothing, you dumb Deutsch tart," I thought, seething at her deliberate treachery. Looking at them both and faking a friendly smile, I said: "Well, ladies, you too seem to be getting along, I'll leave you to it and will go and say Hello to some people I know."

Ignoring Natasha's protests, I headed to another part of the bar and started talking with a nice guy from Surinam who had grown up in the Netherlands and was a successful lawyer at one of the largest firms in the world. The place was starting to fill up and the noise of conversation rose, as did the typical ritual questions and answers that pose as conversations at such events.

"Where are you from?"

"How long have you lived here?"

"What you do?"

"Do you like it here?"

I often think it would save a lot of time if someone simply printed off a set of cards that could be held up as in the Bob Dylan video for "Subterranean Homesick Blues". As questions are being asked, the respondent could simply hold up cards. So, in my case the cards would read:

"London"

"nine years"

"Director of an IT group at McCulloch"

"Hate it, that's why I've lived here for so long."

Another common occurrence at such events is the incessant whining of spoilt Expats (like myself you might say) who do nothing but air a litany of complaints about the Netherlands.

"Do you know that they don't stock my favourite sausages in a single store in the whole of Amsterdam? How crappy is that?"

"It's impossible to get my the brand of soap powder that they have in the UK. It has the same name as the one in the UK but it just doesn't wash as well as when I do it back home. So now I send ALL my washing back to the UK every weekend. Yes it's expensive, but I rather that than have my clothes go through a substandard wash." On and on they go, whining about all the things they can't get here but are available in their home countries.

One of the worst nationalities for this is the French. I love France and French people, when they are in their natural habitat. When French people move abroad, they tend to act as if they are the last surviving members of their people. They cling together like estate agents or bankers, ignore everyone around them and talk in their native language. They are happy to speak English so they can complain about the food, the butchers and the supermarkets, all which of course are vastly superior in France.

If you want to meet a French girl or man (if you must) the best place to do this is at the French bakery in Amsterdam South. It's so popular that people have been known to queue down the road to get at their bread and croissants. There are always lots of single French ladies hanging around there stocking up on the carbs. Forget going to bars and clubs, it's the best pick up place in Amsterdam.

An annoying drunken Latvian girl, skinny as a stick, whose mundane life I once made the mistake of lighting up by having a conversation with her at a previous event came up to me and started giving me a hard time about some jokes that I'd written on my blog: Amsterdamshallowman.com.

Anna had inspired me by calling me shallow and so for a joke I created a blog where I make sarcastic digs at various aspects of life in Amsterdam.

Somehow the Latvian had been offended by a comment I'd made about men hating being dragged along to Museums by their girlfriends.

"You know, your blog about the Museum is not funny. I don't understand it. Why don't men want to go to Museums? It's about upbringing and education, you have to be taught to appreciate art," she slurred. The night was still young and she was already pickled. "Listen, errr" (I couldn't remember her name, she'd made such a huge impact on me last time). "I don't mean to be rude but you're talking, or actually I should say shouting nonsense. I don't need to study art to know what I hate, and one of the things I hate is to be dragged around a Museum with some chick that thinks this is the start of getting her feet under my glass coffee table. Art is entirely subjective, the so-called experts are simply better at spouting bullshit about given subject than the rest of us, nothing more."

I then had to listen to her ranting on about art and culture until I received a tap on my shoulder and was relieved to see that Irina had arrived and in her hand was carrying two glasses of champagne. "Here you are, Simon, I knew you'd be here," she smiled. "You'll need to pay for these at the bar," she added, no surprise there then.

Irina has the dirtiest smile that gets me hard in an instant. She was elegantly dressed in a tight one-piece black dress that ended just below her knees and accentuated her hot body perfectly. Scott was now conversing with a woman of non-descript origin who was so short I feared he'd do permanent damage to his back, the way he was hunched over so they could talk.

Anna, with whom I had an agreement that at such events we should stay away from each other lest people think we're a couple, came over with Natasha, awkward. I introduced Anna to Irina. "So we finally get to meet," said Anna. "Oh, you're Anna, I've heard so much about you," lied Irina, considering I'd barely mentioned Anna to her. "Simon, aren't you going to introduce me to this beautiful woman?" Natasha blushed and reached out her hand to Irina and then responded in Russian to her. They then began to have what sounded to me like a heated discussion in their native language. The only words I could understand were "Natasha, Irina and Simon."

I began to have an uneasy feeling as the two them carried on. "Is everything ok, Simon? You're looking a bit pale.", asked Anna, barely suppressing a laugh. "How privileged I am to be present during one of your nightmares.". I quickly drank the glass of Champagne that Irina had brought me and that I'd had the pleasure of paying for. I excused myself and made an exit, stage left to the bathroom, looking out for any side exits through which I could slip unseen and exit the Hotel. Sadly none were forthcoming.

I have no idea why I felt so uncomfortable with Irina and Natasha. It's not as if I was in a serious relationship with Irina and I'd only just met Natasha. I caught up with some emails while in the bathroom and of course the obligatory Facebook updates. No matter how hard I try, I just can't disable the bloody things on my phone. This time it was a friend of a friend posting a photo of her two dogs in a swimming pool.

I returned to the bar and ordered another glass of champagne plus a bottle of water to prevent a hangover in the morning. I was accosted by Pierre, the world's most boring Belgian, an acquaintance of a former colleague. A conversation with Pierre is like walking through the world in slow motion. Time crawls to a standstill and I wish for death to come and take me as soon as possible rather than endure the torture that is time with Pierre. He should work for the Police. If they have a tough suspect who refuses to admit to a crime, they should lock them in a room with Pierre and I guarantee that they will confess to any crime after five minutes alone with him. I tore myself away as quickly as possible and walked back over to the girls.

Anna was now in conversation with a guy who must have been at least 190 centimeters. Facing away from me Irina and Natasha were now surrounded by the pack of Italian wolves, who were practically foaming at the mouth. My cock was rock hard as I looked at Natasha's glorious figure. She had the kind of arse that countries would fight wars over. The material of her skirt clung to it in ecstasy; I wanted nothing more that moment than to imagine her bent over in front of me with my cock sliding in and out of her while slapping that glorious arse.

I walked into the center of the conversation, which involved one of the Italian guys interrogating Natasha and Irina. "You girls have boyfriend, husband, you single?" he asked in a weasel-like tone of desperation. Natasha, arms folded over her luscious breasts, responded, "Just take a look at us, do you think women like us don't have men?". At that point I walked in between the two girls and looking at the pack of wolves said, "Gentlemen, these faces are leaving now, and sadly you won't be on them.". With that I held the girls' arms and guided them out of the bar and Hotel onto the street.

Natasha turned to me and asked, "So, Simon, you abduct two beautiful girls, what do you have in mind?" "Yes, Simon, what plans do you have for us?" asked Irina with a playful tone in her voice. "Well, as we are in the neighborhood we could go to the Palladium, which is not a long walk away or we could take a taxi," I suggested. This being acceptable to the two girls, and looking like a well-dressed pimp with two of his employees, we walked with both of them holding on to my arms the relatively short distance to the Palladium bar.

As both ladies were wearing killer heels, after a very short distance we stopped a passing Taxi and the three of us squeezed into the back seat. "Where you go?" asked the charming driver. Upon giving the driver the destination he started whining about how it was close enough to walk to and that he'd hardly earned any money all evening. "Listen carefully, you chose to be a taxi driver, I'm sure that a gun wasn't held to your head to force you take this line of work. By choosing to become a taxi driver you've accepted some inherent risks:

1. You might get a passenger that only wants to go a short distance.
2. The passenger in question might report you to taxiklacht.nl if you don't stop complaining and take them to the destination requested."

Upon hearing the name of the website used to forward complaints to City Council which licenses taxi drivers, he immediately stopped complaining and drove us to our destination. I was sat in between Irina and Natasha, who started saying something to each other in Russian. Natasha then leaned into me with an incredibly erotic expression on her face and then stuck her tongue in my mouth. We kissed passionately for about a minute, when Irina not to be left out grabbed me and did the same thing. I then alternated between the two girls while the taxi driver almost ran over cyclists looking back at the show that was going on in the back of his cab. "You disgusting people, where do you think you are? A whorehouse? Get out right now."

Laughing, we exited the taxi which conveniently had stopped just around the corner from our destination. Due to the rudeness of the driver I refused to pay him any money. He drove off shouting, "You whores, you will go to Hell," to which Irina laughed, "If Hell like this, hurry up and take us there."

We had been thrown out of the taxi conveniently close to a chic little bar called Momo. Unusually for Amsterdam this bar and restaurant is a chrome and glass beauty. Great service and generally chic (by Amsterdam standards) crowd. We walked in past the obligatory doormen into the packed bar which was full of aging lions and young and not-so- young antelopes.

We'd only just arrived when, as luck would have it, space opened up on one of the sofas that they have opposite the bar area. Adjacent to the bar are banks of sofas with a coffee table in the middle. The three of us sat down with myself in between the two girls. Opposite us sat two glamorous blonde Dutch ladies in their early forties. Plenty of makeup, Louis Vuitton, Fendi and Chanel as evident as were their loud voices, with one of them talking about doing up the third bathroom in her house in France. She also mentioned how she didn't trust the French and had all building materials shipped in from the Netherlands with Dutch workers doing the job. I'm sure the French locals were not amused.

Rather than waiting hours to get served I pushed my way through the roaring lions and blushing antelopes to the bar where I caught the attention of one of the barmen. I looked over at the girls who were taking photos of each other and themselves, pouting into the camera and no doubt uploading it to Facebook. I proceeded to order a bottle of champagne (what else when with two Russian ladies) plus a bottle of water and some ice. Upon returning to the seat with a waitress carrying the champagne and glasses, Irina and Natasha both shrugged their shoulders in the fashion that told me that this was completely normal and within their expectations.

A waitress poured the champagne and the three of us toasted to a good night out in Amsterdam. I then turned to the ladies and asked, "Have you ever played 'pass the ice cube'?". Intrigued, the ladies responded that they had not. "Well, it's pretty simple, the ice cube has to be passed from each person to the other, no hands allowed and it can't be dropped. Let me demonstrate.". I then took a piece of ice, which I put in my mouth. Reached over to Irina and with my tongue passed the ice cube to her. We kissed passionately and then Irina repeated the same thing with Natasha.

The Dutch ladies opposite looked as if they had just seen a black family moving in next door to them. Their eyes were on stalks and I feared that one of them would be leaving the bar in an ambulance. Natasha now reached over to me and passed me the ice cube with a hot kiss. "Hey, why don't you find a room for that?" said one of the shocked ladies. "You play with us if you like," teased Irina in her sexy voice. "What? We are not playing with you, stop it or I will call the manager and have you thrown out."

"No offence meant, ladies, we're just having some fun but I promise that to protect your sensibilities we'll behave ourselves." I raised my glass to the ladies opposite us then carried on drinking with my hot Russian duo. That's not to say that we were chaste and pure after that. With each glass of champagne we were more touchy-feely, me with the girls and them with each other. "Hey, I have idea, we are in Amsterdam, why we no go see sex?" asked Natasha in a voice loud enough to shock the two Dutch ladies opposite and many people in the vicinity. Agreeing this was a good idea we finished the champagne (both girls drank quickly) and with the admiring looks of some of the lions and a few of the antelopes left Momo hand in hand.

As we left the bar Natasha suggested that we skip the live sex show and head to her place which was nearby. Not one to look a gift horse in the mouth, naturally I accepted her kind offer. To get to her place we needed to walk through the Vondelpark, a huge park in the middle of the city. This place is well-known as an Amsterdam Council-approved gay cruising place after dark. By now it was well past midnight and I was hoping that I wouldn't witness any men having open sex. There were a few drunks and Potheads hanging around. The usual cyclists tearing through the park at night without any lights, but other than that it was pretty quiet.

"Let me show you two something," said Natasha pulling Irina and I in the direction of a secluded spot of the park covered in bushes. She removed her killer heels and continued walking in her bare feet, taking us through some bushes up to a tree. She then leant against it and guided my right hand up under her skirt to a soaking wet pussy. I took Irina's hand and together we began pushing our fingers into Natasha's moist space. I should have known what would happen next as she began moaning and writhing against our combined fingers while Irina and I kissed each other and took turns kissing Natasha.

With a scream that would have woken the dead she shook to

a massive orgasm on our fingers. I took Irina's hand and licked Natasha's juices off her fingers. I fed my wet fingers into Natasha's mouth. Natasha and Irina then both went to their knees and were just starting to unzip the Armani pants when a voice shouted in Dutch, "Hello, hello, is everything ok there?" Turning round I could just make out a flashlight. We quickly readjusted ourselves and came out of the bushes giggling like kids. A policeman on a bike was nearby. "Everything is fine, officer, we just explore the park," said Irina to the policeman with a smile. "Well, why not explore what you want at home, or if you must do it out here, keep the noise down," replied the officer in heavily Dutch accented English. "Sure, will do," I replied, "come on, girls, let's get out of here."

Natasha guided us to her place, only a few minutes from the park itself. On a street with identical-looking terraced houses we entered a small ground apartment up a flight of typical narrow Amsterdam stairs on the first floor. I went to the toilet and while there, heard the girls talking and laughing in Russian. Once out of the bathroom I met the girls who were sitting on an old sofa in the humid living room. I asked Natasha to open the window, which she did. Irina said to me, "Simon, we play game with you.".

"What kind of game?" I asked, my cock hardening at the potential fun ahead. "We'll play a game in a minute, but come here first", I beckoned to the two girls. They came over and the three of us kissed with incredible intensity. They removed my jacked and together stripped me out of my clothes till I was naked.

"Ok, Simon," said Natasha, "Sit on the chair, we have treat for you," she pointed at an old wooden chair. Doing as I was told for once I sat in the chair. "Now put your hands behind your back," asked Irina. I complied and Natasha took what appeared to be a silk rope and tied my hands to the back of the chair with a skill that made it clear that this wasn't the first time that she'd done so. She actually bound my hands quite tightly.

Natasha and Irina now stripped naked and began kissing each other, which was a thing of beauty to behold. They said something in Russian and then both began crawling across the floor together. Like a magician, out of nowhere Natasha produced a small vibrator which she put in Irina's mouth who then licked and sucked on it. Natasha released my penis and began licking it, as did Irina. Natasha took the vibrator and with a single push and a moan slid it into Irina from behind. Irina then began swallowing me whole.

Natasha continued to fuck Irina with the vibrator. I was as hot and turned as I'd ever been when suddenly there was a loud banging on door. "NATASHA, NATASHA, you WHORE, I know you in there, open door." Shit. "What in the name of Bob Marley is going on?" I asked Natasha. "Untie me right now." She ignored me, walked to the door and shouted through the door in Russian. The only word I could understand was 'Dmitry'. "Irina, what's going on? Untie me, I'm getting out of here." Irina who was quickly getting dressed walked past me into the hall and then joined in with Natasha in Russian shouting at the unseen Dmitry.

Suddenly there was a loud crash and what sounded like the door being kicked open. The girls screamed and I did the only thing a natural leader and hero would do. Still tied to the chair I used my well-trained leg muscles to hop backwards until I was close to the living room window that faced onto the street. With all my might and being the scoundrel that I am, prayed to God and then tipped backwards out of the open window from the first floor up into the street.

Luckily for me I landed on a parked car, which broke my fall and the chair. Its alarm went off and I rolled onto the floor. I could hear the unseen Dmitry hollering and the girls screaming. Windows and doors opened to see what was going on. I had such a rush of adrenalin that I leapt up, wearing only my underpants and ran like a madman barefooted through the park. I sprinted for a good ten minutes through the park, passing shocked cyclists and druggies who probably thought they were hallucinating.

I stopped by a park bench and tried to catch my breath. I was unhurt, but barefooted and in Armani boxer shorts. I was just wondering how the Hell I was going to be able to get home dressed like this when out of a nearby set of bushes stepped two men. One was quite chubby and ordinary-looking, while the other appeared to have just stepped off the set of Spartacus. He was in a pair of tight leather pants and not wearing a T-shirt. He had a six-pack and an impressive set of muscles. "Oh, hello there, would you like to join us? We were just playing." I decided to try and be as diplomatic as I could be under the circumstances.

"Actually, you won't believe this but I'm just out for a run." This was the first thing that popped into my head. "Out for a run?" asked Spartacus. "Don't be coy with us, come on into the bushes, let's play." With panic setting in I started backing away slowly. "Oh, he's trying to get away," said Spartacus' overweight partner. "Or are you just one of those bi-curious types out for a tease?" he asked, sweating slightly.

I was just about to sprint when along came the policeman on the bike that had told us off early. "You again," he said looking at me in disbelief. How much sex do you need in one evening?" he asked incredulously. "This is not what it looks like," I replied. "Oh, sure. Put your clothes back on and don't let me see you in this park again tonight, otherwise I'll arrest you and put you in a cell to cool down."

For the second time that evening, I apologized to the policeman and then decided that I had no choice but to try and jog home. Then I remembered that my door keys, phone and wallet were at Natasha's. I really had no choice but to risk the wrath of Dmitry. I explained my predicament to the policeman, who when he'd finished laughing, agreed to accompany me back to Natasha's apartment to make sure that no one had been killed. When we arrived, I could see that my clothes had been thoughtfully thrown out the window and were on the street. Fortunately my wallet and phone were still intact.

The policeman advised me to bugger off home, which I did gratefully, ordering a taxi to take me home frustrated but pleased to be alive and back in the Woolcot palace.

# NIGHTMARES OF A SHALLOW MAN

Midway upon the journey of my life I found myself within a dark forest, they call it the Amsterdamse Bos. My dear sister had warned me that a life of fine wine, women and song could only lead to bad things. If only I'd listened to her.

The last thing I remember was standing on the Roelhof Hartplein after an evening of drinking at the College Hotel. I'd successfully dodged several cyclists that were flying along the pavement while looking at their phones. I recall seeing a scooter rider coming towards me at high speed and then, here I was, standing in the middle of the Amsterdamse Bos.

In front of me stood an old man in a white suit, with a long grey beard and white hair. "Is that a Hugo Boss suit?" I asked. "The brand of the suit is irrelevant, your obsession with all things shallow and material has led you to be where you are now.".

The old man took me through a large set of iron doors behind which were a set of stairs. Down we walked for what seemed like ages until we reached the first level. "You lived a life dominated by carnal desires, vanities and conspicuous consumption." He opened another set of doors. Suddenly I appeared to be in the PC Hooftstraat a place I knew well. It looked exactly the same apart from the fact that the old man and I were the only people on the street and it was eerily quiet.

I decided to pop into some of my favorite stores, starting with the ICI Paris to buy some of my usual Chanel face cream and some appropriately named Egoiste after- shave. As I entered the store I realised that something was definitely not quite right. All of the usually elegantly dressed staff were wearing jeans, a nondescript leopard skin- patterned top and all three women that worked in the store had wet hair. Even worse they all had cigarettes in their mouths and were smoking while also intermittently checking their smartphones. I walked out of the store in disgust.

I walked further on, planning to cross over the road to go into the Church's shoe store. Now suddenly a horde of cyclists rode along, all were in jeans and texting while cycling. I managed to cross the road unscathed and entered the store. Again it was staffed by women wearing jeans. Their hair was wet, they were smoking and texting, shouting loudly at each other, smoking and texting. I left, shell- shocked and as I entered multiple stores, the same story repeated itself. Women with wet hair, jeans, cigarettes, irresponsible cyclists. "I've got to get out of here," I said to the old man. "No problem at all," said he and with a wave of his hand suddenly a taxi appeared. We got in and I said to the driver "take me to the Dylan Hotel, I need a drink." "The Dylan hotel?" asked the taxi driver, "you'll need to direct me, I don't know where that is," he said. I held my tongue and started to give him directions. The radio in the taxi was turned up loud and was playing a dreadful song by Lady Gaga (aren't they all awful?); I think it was called Poker Face.

I asked him to turn it down and he ignored me. We'd only just left the PC Hooftstraat and yet the meter was turning over at high speed and was already at 15 Euros. "What's wrong with your meter?" I asked. "It's already 15 Euros and we've barely moved." The driver threw back his head and laughed and laughed, "the price is what it says on the meter, I can do nothing about it." The journey to Vinkeles took forever and the Lady Gaga song played over and over again.

I saw that we passed through the Rembrandt Plein and past Central Station. "You're taking the long way round to the destination," I said. "These are not the directions I gave you.". Again he laughed and shrugged his shoulders. We arrived at the Dylan Hotel and the price on the meter was 55 Euros. I was so happy to get out of the taxi that I just paid without any further complaint.

We walked into the Hotel bar and I knew something wasn't right, the usually elegant crowd in the bar was full of men with identical bad hairstyles, cheap suits and brown shoes. The women all had wet hair, were wearing jeans and badly colour-coordinated tops. They were all smoking and texting. The noise levels were incredible; I went to the bar and tried to order a drink but the barman was busy with his smartphone and no matter how much I tried to get his attention he just ignored me.

I looked at the old man and said, "What's going on, why is everything like this?" He smiled and said, "How you lived and judged others is how you'll spend eternity, welcome to Hell."

# JULY 7TH

I awoke somewhat shaken and definitely stirred from the previous night's events and the bizarre nightmare. I felt like the man who won a million on the lottery only to lose the ticket on the way to the shop to claim his loot. I really had hit the jackpot, two hot Russian women, hot-to-trot and yet there I was, alone and frustrated in my bed.

After some do-it-yourself sexual healing with the help of some German porn I decided that I needed to take things easy. Irina called me to explain that Dmitry was Natasha's estranged husband and that after a huge and furious argument they had kissed and made up. Irina had the sense to throw my clothes out the window to avoid Dmitry seeing them. She had left soon after. She was not too impressed at my stuntman escapades and decided that she wanted some Woolcot-free time, which was fine by me. I spent most of the day being killed by teenagers online on Call of Duty Black Ops on the PlayStation. Managed to tear myself away long enough to go for a 20 kilometer run along the Amstel river. Returned home and spent the rest of the day alternatively listening to music or being on the PlayStation. Suitably recovered, I even made time for some top quality German porn, avoiding any titles that involved male and female threesomes for obvious reasons.

# HOW TO DATE DUTCH WOMEN

Having lived here since the time when Geert Wilders had normal hair, the Dutch football team were actually capable of winning football matches and Carice Van Houten wasn't the only Dutch celebrity, a lot of Expats see me as a kind of father figure and come to me for advice on many matters. Over the years one particular theme has cropped up repeatedly; how to date Dutch women.

The young Expats come to me with tears in their eyes and say, "Shallow Man, we have no problem dating Italians, Germans, French, Russians, Latvians and Polish girls. When absolutely desperate we even date British girls, but the Dutch? Why are they so difficult?"

Having had some experience in this area and even though what I'm about to write may be somewhat controversial in some quarters, like John the Baptist I feel that the truth must be told, and if as a result my head is served on a plate at FEBO or in a food hall at HEMA then so be it. The things I do for my readers.

Every woman is different, so of course I will have to generalise. The tips I will provide are just ways of helping to at least get as far as a good conversation or better still the things that Expat men should not say to Dutch women.

## Religion

To get anywhere with a Dutch woman you have to be able to understand, respect and tolerate their primary religion which is smoking. Dutch women worship smoking above just about anything else. Take a wander through the Pijp or the nine streets on a freezing cold day when even the penguins are wearing Burberry scarves, hats and gloves. The only people you'll see outside the bars on those days will be Dutch women desperately smoking as if cigarettes are about to be prohibited and it's their last chance to ever smoke again.

To get past the basic niceties of an introduction it will not help if you make comments about smoking being detrimental to their health or commenting on why they are either in the freezing cold smoking or asking them not to smoke inside a busy bar as there is a smoking ban. If you can hold your tongue you'll be on to first base.

## Jeans

Learn from my past mistakes. Never, even after a glass of champagne or four, make jokes about the tendency of Dutch women to wear jeans morning, noon and night, at weddings, funerals, Michelin star restaurants, exhibitions, art galleries, private parties etc. This will get you instantly dismissed from any further conversation. Many Amsterdammer's are firm believers in the Dutch philosophy of "Doe Maar Normal". Which translated means, "do not dare to display any individuality at all." Be a clone, if the next 50 women are wearing jeans then so should you.

## Equality and Dutch women

Do not, under any circumstances bring up the subject of part time working. It's a love killer. 90% of Dutch women work part-time. In Dutch society a lot of women believe that not cutting their hair, shouting loudly and acting aggressively makes them liberated. In fact financial independence is one of the strongest indicators of equality. Sadly, most Dutch women in a relationship contribute less than a quarter of the household income.

The Dutch taxpayer (including me) pays a fortune every year for thousands of women to go to University and get a degree. Often women only work full-time for several years and then as soon as they find a man go part-time, something which is allowed under Dutch employment law. This leads to the ridiculous situation where it's common to receive out of office replies from female colleagues that say things such as:

"I work Mondays till 2.12 pm, Wednesdays till 1 pm, Thursdays till 2.47 and Fridays I'm not in the office."

Just nod your head and smile when they tell you how independent Dutch women are.

## Ik Ga Plassen

Some Dutch ladies are in the habit of announcing in a loud voice that they are going for a piss. The literal translation of "Ik ga plassen." When this happens, don't look embarrassed or disgusted. Act as if it's perfectly normal for an adult female to announce to the world what she is about to do in the toilet. Lovely!

## When speaking in English

Speak clearly! My fellow Brits are the worst people for this. In fact a German colleague of mine once had this to say.

"If you have a meeting with a German, a Frenchman and an Indian all three will have the meeting in English and have no problems with communication at all. If a native English speaker joins everyone is confused."

Brits in particular, but also Aussies and Americans, have a habit of talking at the same speed that they use when talking to friends and family in their own countries. In spite of the fact that most non-native English speakers tend to have better grammar than the natives, just because the Dutch can speak good English does not mean that you can talk at them at a rate of 30 words a minute and expect them to understand you. This is often why native speakers fail when talking to Dutch women. Slow down, pronounce your words, use syllables and pauses.

All of the above tips are copyrighted by the Shallow Man.

No Dutch ladies were hurt during the writing of this article.

Now I need to get back to GTA V. Till next time, Hou je bek.

# BOOK 2, THE BOOK OF GREED

# JULY 8$^{TH}$

Back in the office again at McCulloch where a panic is ensuing due to the impending visit the following morning of Christian. Oh joy. After a day of the usual justifying the unjustifiable, convinced Koen to join me for a quick drink after work, which turned into dinner at the LaVina Experience in the Rivierenburt area of Amsterdam.

Over a quality meal we discussed all the latest office gossip and after we'd started on our second bottle of wine Koen let slip that his salary was a staggering 135,000 Euros a year. Ten thousand a year more than myself, un-bloody- believable. I, of course, did not let on that he earned more than me, and may even have hinted that I earned more.

In spite of his initial reservations, managed to convince him to take a Monday night visit to my favorite strip bar in Amsterdam in the middle of the Red Light District, Brave Meisjes. A seedy little place, hidden away behind an incredibly narrow backstreet of the Red Light area. As we squeezed our way past gawking tourists with eyes as wide as the legs of a promiscuous woman, I have to admit that there were certainly some hot women working that night. One in particular caught my eye. A fit-looking blonde with huge natural breasts and a bikini that was so thin it might as well have been made out of dental floss. A group of guys were hanging around in front of the window, egging each other on to go and sample her, no doubt, well-rehearsed and passionless delights.

We walked on giving points to the various delicacies on display in the red light windows. "Don't like the look of yours much," I commented to Koen as a woman who looked as if she'd been a sparring partner for George Foreman gestured at us to join her. "Come, guys, I can take two at a time, no problem." I had no problem believing her, she was the living embodiment of the old song from the Specials, 'Too Much Too Young.' We politely passed on her kind offer and headed to the strip bar. A bored-looking bouncer let us in after relieving us of 10 Euros each for the entrance fee.

There are many cynical people out there who say that multiculturalism is a bad thing and that we humans are simply too stuck in our ways to get along properly. One of the exceptions to this is the microcosm of the strip bar. We entered the main narrow, neon-lit room, which had one long bar going through the center and another smaller one in the corner, upon which an M&M multi-colored selection of women danced topless.

Meanwhile seated at the bar was a cross-section of races and nationalities all huddled together in harmony, dry of tongue and wide of eye, taking in the dubious delights of cultural entertainment that evening.

A twitchy-looking gentleman of Asian appearance waved a 20 Euro note at a rather tough-looking lady covered in tattoos, who was shaking her not inconsiderable assets on the top of the bar to some dreadful song with a pounding beat.

With a false smile, she snatched the money from his hand, faster than a man in a suit leaving a lady's room in the Red Light District. She then waited for the next song to start, sat on his lap and began writhing on top of him.

He looked as if he was about to faint from happiness or horniness, take your pick. "I thought Silicon Valley was supposed to be in the US," I said to Koen as loudly as I could without risking taking a beating from one of the security staff. "I don't think that any of the women working here has natural breasts," replied Koen, taking in the sights of the five or six ladies working that evening.

Meanwhile back at the bar, the Asian chap was now licking and sucking on the nipples of his hired partner. He squeezed them as if they were a raft in the middle of a lonely sea, which in reality to him they probably were. He grasped, groped, licked and sucked as much as he could get, when suddenly the dreadful song was over. Koen and I, drinking beer at 6 Euros a bottle observed fascinated as the dancer asked him if he'd like another go. He declined and with a cold and dismissive stare followed by another false smile, she moved over to a brown-skinned chap sitting a couple seats away who was waving 20 Euros at her. She repeated the same false smile, sit-on-the-lap routine while her former three-minute-partner looked ruefully on..

The new partner of the stripper wasted no time getting straight to business and sucked on her nipples as if he were seriously dehydrated and was desperate for a drink. "Ouch! Don't bite," warned the stripper as her partner was obviously hungry as well as thirsty. "I wonder how many food poisoning outbreaks have started here," pondered Koen. "You have a good point," I responded, unable to take my eyes of the sucking and biting show playing out before me. "If she gets through nine or ten guys a night, all slobbering over her breasts, just think of the bacteria being passed from mouth to nipple to the next mouth, what a horrible thought."

As we were talking a succession of ladies working in the bar approached us asking if we'd like a lap dance. Being a man of steel and a sucker for beautiful women, and because the only attractive lady working that night - Leonie - gave me such a sexy, genuine smile I couldn't resist. Her smile wasn't the only genuine thing about her, she had a pair of breasts that were so good and naturel, that if they sold them on Amazon, I'd be placing orders every day.

I took the place at the bar of a chubby-looking guy whom the lovely Leonie had told to vacate the seat. With a cold smile that melted as soon as I handed over 20 Euros, she waited until another Europop song with a pounding beat came on, and she was off. She hopped into my lap, with her legs spread over my cock and began grinding slowly on it. She grabbed her breasts, that were still glistening with the saliva of her previous partner and motioned at my head to come forward and feast on them. This was the last thing that I wanted to do, so I actually backed away from her. "Why don't you suck them, they're very tasty," she said with a lascivious smile. "No thanks," I responded, "do you perhaps have any hygiene wipes you could use on them first?"

She suddenly stopped her grinding in my lap and this was not the first time I realized how a mouse must feel when cornered by a hungry cat.

"Hygiene wipes?" she shouted, "Hygiene wipes?" As she said this a sliver of ice ran down my back, I felt my heart beating as if I'd just sprinted my way through a 10 kilometer race, I tensed up and felt pressure building in my ears. Every nerve in my body tingled and I was on red alert. "Hahhahahahahah," she roared, suddenly throwing her arms around me, "that's brilliant.".

She then shouted at the other strippers and repeated my statement to them in Dutch. The girls all laughed and some of the guys looked at me with angry stares, not pleased at having their 20 Euro nighttime snacks interrupted by the obviously amusing comments of the best dressed man in the bar. "I love a man with a sense of humor,", said Leonie to me; she obviously thought I was joking about the wipes. By this time the song (if you could call it that) was almost over, which is a good point. Some so-called songs nowadays are so dreadful and sound so similar that how in the name of Bob Marley do the DJ's know when one ends and the next one begins? I digress. So being the ever polite English gentleman I then paid for another dance with the lovely Leonie, who – luckily - was dumb enough to take my request for a saliva and bacteria-free pair of breasts as a joke.

Lucky me, since I wasn't in the mood to face being thrown out of my second Red Light establishment in less than a week.

In spite of being requested to grab and play with her not inconsiderable assets, I remained polite and kept my hands only on her waist. This seemed to confuse her and even cause some distress. "Is there something wrong with me? Are my tits too big for you?" she asked worriedly. I assured her that there was no such thing (within reason) of boobs being too large. I simply lied through my teeth and said that I thought it was somewhat disrespectful to grope and suck a lady's breasts as if they were a combined watering hole and mango tree in the middle of the Sahara. (Desert, not nightclub.)

Leonie, perturbed by my perceived lack of interest in her natural assets (you should have seen them, they were spectacular) decided that she had to see how I'd behave in private and after the dance had finished, came by to where Koen and I were standing and subtly slipped a card with her phone number in one of the pockets of my beautiful suit.

"She likes you," said Koen with something bordering on admiration. "It's the Woolcot charm, it's like a Dutch woman's Smartphone, never turned off."

We left the breast-feeding station for adult men (or strip club) and finally after a long and reassuringly expensive night, headed for home.

# MORE TIPS FROM THE DUTCH DATING SCENE

In Amsterdam's famous street market, the Albert Cuyp there were two fish stalls situated next to each other, one which was run by a man and the other by a woman.

One typical Amsterdam Saturday afternoon, in the middle of the market, teeming with people desperate to get their hands on some cheap herring, fake razor blades and all manner of counterfeit products, an unscrupulous chap snatched a lady's handbag and ran away through the madding crowd. A policeman laid chase and in panic, the bag snatcher ran straight into the middle of both fish stalls, knocking over most of the stock onto the floor. As the stall holders were picking up the fish from the floor (to go immediately back on sale) they both held on to a single piece of fish at the same time. Looking deeply into the eyes of the female stallholder, the male stallholder asked, "Your plaice or mine?"; which brings me to the subject of today's article.

The Shallow Man, gifted with good manners, exceptional taste in clothes and that rare thing in these times of austerity - a keen sense of humor - has gathered plenty of experience in dating our wet-haired, denim-clad hosts. Since the previous post on how to date Dutch men and women, the Shallow Man has been inundated with requests for further information on how to snare that most desired of prey, the Dutch. In spite of the inevitable backlash that will come as surely as the entire Kardashian family have no talent, I will again don my favorite Teflon suit and enter once more into the intercultural breach. The things I do for my readers!

**Thank God It's Friday!!**

It's a well-known fact in the Netherlands that the majority of children are conceived on a Friday night. This is due to the fact that at the end of the working week (12-16 hours for the average woman) the majority of Dutch singles (or people away from their partners for the evening) have a rush of hormones, testosterone or plain Dutch courage fuelled by toxic Eetcafe cheap wine and beer and are suddenly - for a small window of time - full of the joys of the world and open for adventures of the flirting kind.

## Places To Watch The Dutch Mating Game In All Of Its Denim-Clad Glory

Being bound to Amsterdam like Yolanthe to Wesley Sneijder, the Shallow Man will provide local advice. However the same probably applies to most Dutch cities.

### De Duvel Or Other Busy Eetcafes

In the establishment above, beer and wine are cheap, food is good and so are the customers (cheap or good, take your pick). In order to get into the swing of a Friday night at De Duvel, the Shallow Man advises to book a table and eat there. It's then pretty easy to stakeout which tables are filled with groups of singles. After 10 pm, the music is turned up and the bar turns into an Amsterdam version of various species of animals hanging around by the watering hole.

Hungry young lions, easily identifiable by their Simba- like hair, blue or red jeans and brown shoes are stalked by the world's most ferocious antelopes. In the hunting ground that is the Amsterdam dating scene, it's the women who wear the trousers (or jeans and cheap boots) and select their victims with the precision of Jack the Ripper on a wander through Whitechapel on a dark night.

In the Dutch dating scene it's all about proximity. Stand at a packed bar and if the women are interested they will go after the man in question like our ancestors, the cavemen of old. With a none-too-subtle wave of the club, they will literally whack their prey over the head and drag them back to the cave for a night of vigorous aerobics or at least, if the prey survives the intense questioning about where they're from, job, why they don't speak Dutch etc., get a phone number and an opportunity for a crack at the assets at a later date.

Dutch women tend to be extremely loud and are incredibly talented. If three Dutch women are sat together or standing by each other in a bar, they will shout at each other at the top of their voices simultaneously and yet understand each other perfectly, which in itself is a much underrated talent.

## Don't Scare The Lions Or The Antelopes

The lions may stand by the watering hole, drinking beer, looking around, drinking beer, looking around, but it's the antelopes that are in control. Dutch men will stand together in groups, while even the tastiest, juiciest example of antelope trots by in denim with unstyled hair, unmolested. The antelopes, once they've finished shouting at each other, checking their smartphones and announcing, 'IK GA PLASSEN', then select the lion worth talking to and make their move. Again as I stated earlier, proximity is everything. Stand by the antelope or the lions and you may stand a chance to be noticed, hunted and scooped up. Don't make either species nervous by being too well- dressed.

## Be Humble, Uriah, Be Humble

The Shallow Man does not take lightly to having women who are dressed as if they just spent the night sleeping on a friend's sofa and haven't bothered changing, attempting to talk down to him in a mock posh accent. However, if you really are looking for success with the species, better be humble and allow yourself to be patronised by someone whose entire outfit costs less than the boxer shorts worn by the Shallow Man.

## How To Win The Heart Of Your Dutchie On The First Date

If you are on a date with a Dutch woman for the first time and wish to make an impression, bring along a packet of cigarettes and hand it over to her; it will be love at first cough.

If you wish to impress the Dutch male, drop a 5 Euro note just behind where he's sitting, then ask, "Is that yours?" He will be so overjoyed with happiness for the rest of the evening that he'll be like Hagelslag in your hands. He might even settle the bill, however I'd suggest dropping a 10 Euro note to really make him ecstatic.

The tips above are of course a generalisation, because as we all know the Dutch rarely go out wearing jeans, smoke and have hair that is unstyled.

No antelopes or lions were hurt during the writing of this article.

# JULY 9$^{TH}$ OR GIMME ME SOME MORE

At the fine offices of McCulloch, those members of Christian's management team based in Amsterdam normally enter the office between 9 and 10.

Due to my challenging and active social and love life, I rarely visit the office before 10. However, on this fated day, Christian, he of the never-ending monologues and tedious art of conversation would be visiting us for a team meeting and one-on-one goal setting sessions. Knowing his penchant for arriving as early as possible, I made a supreme effort and arrived in the office at a record-setting 8. 30 in the morning.

I was determined to discuss the subject of a pay rise with him. Koen was on 10,000 Euros a year more than me, disgraceful. This had to be addressed. My honour was at stake here. It's not even as if Koen spends his money on anything tangible. He wears off-the-peg Tommy Hilfiger suits (the less said about that the better) and non-descript, made-in-China shoes from some old Dutch brand that no one from a country with more that ten people has ever heard of.

The team meeting went against the usual convention of the old saying that there is no 'I' in team. Christian, after a 45 minute introduction, spent the rest of the 3 hour meeting torturing us with a collection of PowerPoint slides and Excel sheets. Christian has 4 direct reports, myself and Koen in Amsterdam. In Hong Kong sits the world's most irritating woman, Cindy Li, who has a habit of ending every sentence with "You agree with me, right?" She is so good at kissing Christian's arse that she must see the world through a shade of brown. In New York sat the other member of his management team, Bernadette, who looked after our supplier management activities on his behalf and who - rumor had it - was also a part-time hit woman for the five mafia families in New York, but that was of course unproven.

The meeting was the typical unproductive gathering that I've been used to at McCulloch. Whenever Christian allowed someone to speak, he usually interrupted or even worse, Cindy Li would talk and talk, repeating the same points, then asking, "You agree with what I'm saying, right?". This was followed by Christian's incessant droning on. The corporate game is a tedious but predictable one. His team members want to impress him, he wants to impress his other Partners, they wish to impress their clients.

Have you ever noticed how, when the most senior guy in the room tells a joke, the weaker of characters fall over themselves to laugh as if it was the funniest thing ever said? Christian with his heavy German accent and droning speaking style is hardly the Eddie Murphy of the business world. This didn't stop Koen, Cindy and even Bernadette from laughing as if they were in the middle of a Richard Pryor act.

Had lunch with Christian and the team. This, due to the recession, was typical Dutch food. Bitterballen, deep fried muck that a cat would turn its nose up at, and that most delightful of food, cheese and tomato sandwiches made with bread that was so hard, single ladies were known to carry it around with them in their handbags at night and use it for self-defense in the event of being attacked.

Managed to get Christian on his own to have a serious discussion with him about my salary. "What are you saying, Simon? That you don't get paid enough? You are having a very good salary, no? " asked Christian incredulously. "The point, Christian, is not whether the salary in itself, in macroeconomic terms can be defined as at or above the median salary for a position of my level, which indeed could be construed as being absolutely necessary for McCulloch to attract and retain exceptional resources, vis-à-vis me. The question is from your perspective, are you rewarding and compensating me adequately for the services and results that I provide?"

Looking somewhat confused and exasperated, Christian responded, "Simon, you are paid more than enough, and in the current economic climate, I am not justifying a pay rise for you, ja?". I tried several other long-winded arguments, but to no avail. Christian was like a Dutch woman on a first date, the legs were being kept firmly crossed. Dispirited and annoyed, I then had to listen to him berating me for turning up late for the meeting in Paris, smelling of booze and looking like death. "Simon, you are not 21 anymore, ja? You must be more professional. You English guys always drink too much and too quickly; slow down and make sure you attend meetings on time."

Well and truly ticked off, he also reminded me that we'd be in Paris for two days later in the week and he expected me to be sober and alert. I almost felt like reminding him that as far as I was aware he was not my father. I resisted the temptation of doing so and left his office in a foul mood.

# THE SHALLOW MAN'S GUIDE TO AMSTERDAM PART 1

Having safely returned from Het Gooi, the Shallow Man paid a visit to an exclusive HiFi store to look at upgrading his state -of -the -art home entertainment system. The store is so expensive that they offer their customers a glass of champagne on entering. They also have private listening rooms where one can listen to various HiFi components in comfort. I entered one of the demo rooms and the salesman explained an array of complex and reassuringly expensive gadgetry to me. "In front of you, sir, you see a pair of state -of -the -art front speakers. In the middle, a pre-amplifier, power amp, digital audio converter and a streamer." Next to all of this equipment, sat in the corner was a dog wearing a gimp mask, and covered in leather. It was chained to one of the amplifiers.

"What's that?" I asked the salesman.

"That, sir, is a subwoofer."

The notoriety and reputation of the Shallow Man for guiding and advising the Expat community of the Netherlands has spread far and wide. I can barely access my inbox, so full is it from requests for advice from not only people based here, but also from those who are about to move to Amsterdam.

I'm honored that my advice is well -received, regardless of the consequences to my perfectly tailored self. Recently, the Shallow Man has received a number of questions about that fair city to the North of Holland, Amsterdam. I've been asked: "Shallow Man, I will shortly be moving to Amsterdam, and, while probably not worthy of living in the same neighborhood as yourself, would at least like some impartial advice on where in Amsterdam I should live."

While unable to provide advice for being vertically challenged (shortly moving to Amsterdam), I can indeed assist with where one should live in the city where red traffic lights exist only for decoration and jeans are mandatory.

Many Amsterdammer's have their own view of what constitutes the best neighbourhoods in the Dam. The Shallow Man will risk the criticism and anger of various cheap -suited estate agents, grasping property owners and so -called experts, and deliver his own advice on where to live in Amsterdam. If as a result I am tied to a chair and force -fed raw herring while watching endless replays of the crowning of Willem Alexander and his wife from Argentina, then I'll face it and shout out "doe maar". The things I do for my readers!

It will not be possible to do justice to this fair city in a single post, so today the Shallow Man will focus on the following two areas of Amsterdam.

## Amsterdam Zuid Oost

If you are looking to move into an area of Amsterdam where you will do a lot of sport and thus lose weight as a result, the Shallow Man strongly recommends moving to the Southeast part of the city. Due to the risk of being robbed, you will find yourself jogging or sprinting on a regular basis, which can only be good for the cardiovascular condition. "Where are the Police?" one might ask. They have a considerable presence and always go everywhere in pairs. Inside the Police station. Whereas many parts of the Netherlands continue to feel the effects of the recession, I have it on good authority that the sales of bullet proof vests, home security and pit bulls continue to do well there. The properties in the neighborhood are built to last, from the finest concrete money can buy. There are good public transport connections using the metro, that has the delicious smell of heavily saturated fats and fried chicken. Lekker!

There are many local artists based there, as can be witnessed by the vast amount of graffiti in just about every street. If you like football or going to concerts, the main arena and Ziggo dome are nearby. You will never be bored in Amsterdam Zuid Oost, excitement is guaranteed.

## Amsterdam East

The Shallow Man was once cast out into the wilderness by an angry Russian ex-girlfriend, and, for some time (if felt like forty days and forty nights), wandered through the desolate and depressing landscape that is Amsterdam East. If, like Ebenezer Scrooge, you prefer splendid isolation, then Amsterdam East is for you. It is in the wrong end of the world. The smell of kebab and other fast food fills the air, like the smell of sweat and smoke in an Amsterdam Bar after 11 pm. If you are female and in need of compliments you'll feel right at home there, as it's barely possible to walk from one end of a street to another without encouraging shouts of "Schatje, Schatje "(sweety) or "hoer" (whore). What's also common is for women to be hissed at like female members of the snake family. If you enjoy being alone and would like to discourage unwanted visitors, this is the perfect part of Amsterdam to live, as most people won't go anywhere near Amsterdam East after 7pm. On the plus side, there is the Oosterpark, where many festivals take place during summertime. The Oosterpark is particularly popular with Romanian pickpockets, drug dealers and trainee doctors looking to get hands-on ER experience. The Harbor club, a place that believes firmly in style over substance, is also situated at the very end of Amsterdam East. Many fine cars can be seen driving rapidly through the neighborhood to that location. They then drive at high speed back to the more civilized areas such as Amsterdam Zuid, the Jordaan or Amstelveen.

No drug dealers, gun runners or snakes were hurt during the writing of this article.

# JULY 10TH

A day of tedium at work. Did my best to be pleasant to Koen, that overpaid snake. How can it be that he earns more than me? Totally outrageous. Of course I smiled at him and made nice, but I'm seriously not amused. Koen is a man that you can set your Rolex by. He's in at 8.30 every day and gone at 5pm on the dot. The only time I've ever known him to stay late was when there was snow everywhere and he decided to wait until the traffic had died down.

The way he dresses! The man earns a fortune and yet still buys his suits off the peg from Hugo Boss. I wouldn't hire such a person, let alone pay him an outrageous salary. "Vengeance is mine," said the Lord, and I intend to get some.

I have no idea what's going on in Amsterdam at the moment. My Dutch is good enough to read the local media and there has been a spate of gangland shootings going on lately. Fortunately, most of the action takes place in the Amsterdam lesser neighborhoods of East and Southeast and even Amsterdam Bos en Lommer, all situated well outside of my social circle.

After a day of being talked at by Christian, I decided that some stress relief was needed. I gave Lieke, a Dutch former project assistant and graduate trainee at McCulloch a call. Lieke was a mass of inconsistencies wrapped up in a hot body, with the face of an angel and the temper and passion of a demon. It goes without saying that even though I was in a relationship with the psychotic Lucy at the time, this didn't stop me from pursuing Lieke like a fox chasing after a chicken. She was a woman who couldn't make her mind up from one minute to the next. I use the term woman loosely  as she's actually twenty years younger than me. The first time I asked her out on a date it took her three weeks to give me an answer. In fact by the time she agreed, I'd almost forgotten that I'd asked her in the first place. As I was determined to get her out of her red hot outfit in record time, I did something I never normally do on a first date. I took her to Ciel Bleu, at the Hotel Okura. This is one of the best eateries in the country and has two Michelin stars. Unfortunately my plan backfired as being Dutch and from a humble background, she was intimidated by the opulence, grand service and stunning view from the 23rd floor of the Hotel.

Have you ever tried holding a sparrow in your hands? That's how I'd describe Lieke. After dinner we had a passionate kiss. She then freaked out and in the way that only Dutch girls can, in spite of wearing high heels and a slinky black dress (oh, I'd have given anything to be in its place) hopped onto her bike and cycled away at high speed.

This was followed by some awkward stilted conversation at work and much blushing on her part. I'd given up hope of ever unlocking her womanly pleasures until months later, when out of the blue she sent me an email and asked to meet after work. To cut a long story short, we ended up shagging each other's brains out. A long, hot, sweaty night in her student-like pad, that she shared with four other people in the desolate wasteland is known as Amsterdam East. Following that, she played hot and cold again like a bank manager losing interest after a withdrawal.

Once in awhile, we repeated this pattern. Not speaking for months at a time, followed by a hot passionate fling, then radio silence again. I knew that meeting her usually was a guarantee for either hot sex or an evening of arguing. Some people get their kicks by going to a casino, I just give Lieke a call.

Anna of course followed my adventures with various women, including Lieke with an exasperated shake of the head, and spoke to me like a teacher correcting a naughty pupil. I visited her at her desk and told her about the evening's assignation, to which she shooed me away angrily. "How much is enough for you, Simon?" she asked, obviously annoyed with me for some reason. "You'll never learn will you?"

Ignoring the whining of the Fraeulein who was obviously determined to worsen my mood, I decided to pay a visit to my tailors, Pakkend, who were conveniently located close to where I lived.

I was greeted with a genuine warm welcome by Casper, one of the owners who took me through some of the latest fabrics they'd just got in. One of the joys in life is selecting a bespoke made suit. Choosing the various options, including lining and what you'd like in writing on the lining. For example, if I listened to Anna, I would have Shallow Man stitched onto the label.

Went through the various options that also included the width of the lapel. As I am currently influenced by Don Draper from Mad Men, I tend to go for the thinnest one possible. I have a penchant for single-breasted suits, with a narrow cut for the trousers. Chose the buttons and went for a single button, plus a waistcoat with high lapels as worn by Sean Connery in Goldfinger, probably the best suit worn by anyone ever, period.

Opting for a navy blue Scabal number, with a flash of the Platinum card ordered my latest three piece bespoke masterpiece and a stunning silk tie to match. I estimate that I probably spend between 4 to 5 thousand Euros a year on bespoke suits, money well spent, as I look like a King and women and the public in general can do nothing but worship me. Or at least give me admiring or hateful glances, take your pick.

With a spring in my step, I headed off in the direction of the Apollolaan Hilton Hotel, to meet the unpredictable Lieke at Roberto's, my favorite Italian restaurant in Amsterdam. The Hotel is the same mentioned in the Beatles song, "The Ballad Of John and Yoko". It was where John and Yoko had their bed-in for world peace. I was also interested in peace, a piece of Lieke.

I took my seat at a table on the terrace and waited impatiently for her to arrive. When she did turn up, fifteen minutes late, I can say it was well worth the wait. She wore skin tight satin-type leggings and a skimpy black shoulderless top that just covered her breasts, which were very healthy indeed. My penis immediately stood to attention. Lieke greeted me with a kiss on the cheeks.

Upon sitting down, she spoke breathlessly in a high pitched voice without pausing, "I didn't kiss you properly as I'm not ready for that yet. You know I like you but we're not just going to kiss, it's been ages. I can see that you're disappointed but that's just how it's going to have to be." I attempted to get a word in edgeways to explain to her that I really wasn't bothered about kissing her, but on she went in this vein throughout what was actually an outstanding meal.

In particular the Lobster Ravioli followed by Sea Bass cooked in a salted crust were both first class.

"So that you know, almost every time we meet we end up having sex and I like the sex you know, but you never call me afterwards, or try and arrange anything; anyway I'm not sure if we could have a relationship due to our age difference, I'd like children at some stage, and having such an old man being the father to the children wouldn't be good.

The thing is, Simon, I've been seeing this new guy I like, he listens to me and we have a good time together, but I'm not sure if he's the right man for me, he likes me and I like him, and we spend lots of time together, but he's a teacher, and teaching doesn't pay well, and who knows, with all the Government cuts, he might not keep his job. I want him to do something else, but he's so lazy, he won't change and tells me he likes the holidays that come with the job, but I said to him…"

On and on and on she went. Now I knew how a terrorist felt when hearing an oncoming drone sent by the US to kill him and everyone in the village.

I decided to ignore the old man comment and with anger rising within me I set out to put her straight on a couple of things. "Lieke, just because I'm not interested doesn't mean that I don't care. You're the one who likes playing stupid games. We have sex, we talk, we don't talk, we have sex. The problem with you is that you don't know what you want. Sex is what I want from you, not a relationship and certainly not children. You're too young, and quite frankly a bit of a pain in the arse." At that point, Lieke threw a glass of perfectly good Barolo (she was having veal) over my magnificent, handmade black bespoke suit and stormed off. A smirking waiter helped me wipe the wine off my suit, "Hey, that's women for you sir, she's a wild one." I couldn't have put it better myself.

Frustrated and fearful for the future of my exquisite suit, I headed back to the Woolcot palace to relieve myself with the aid of some quality pornography. I also needed to pack as I had an early train to Paris the next day.

# THE SHALLOW MAN'S GUIDE TO AMSTERDAM WEST

The Shallow Man looks fondly back at the eighties as a time of bright colors, shoulder pads, Dynasty (What a chap Blake Carrington was!) and, of course, the rise of the King of pop, Michael Jackson. I was there in the crowd at Wembley Stadium in the summer of 1988 along with 70,000 wonderful people watching MJ moonwalk across the stage. Happy memories. Having lived through that period, I was none too excited to be invited to a 1980's party, however, against my better judgment, the Shallow Man attended. I'd forgotten quite how many dreadful songs were popular during this period, and for good reason. Mel and Kim? Bananarama? Kim Wilde sang a song which had the line 'view from a bridge, can't take anymore,' well that's exactly how I felt hearing that song. Another annoying song I'd forgotten was called "We Close Our Eyes". What an irritating number, sung by a group called Go West, which brings me to the subject of today's post.

A common request received by the Shallow Man is for advice on where to live in Amsterdam. I've already provided my frank and uncensored views of Amsterdam East and Southeast.

My views have been duly noted and have caused upset in some quarters. Undaunted by criticism, I will press on, like the Tolpuddle Martyrs of old, with my reviews of Amsterdam. Today I will review Amsterdam West. If as a result I am handcuffed to a chair and forced to sit through repeated showings of Soldat van Oranje while being force -fed Zuurkool, (Sauerkraut) I will be bold and shout out

"I am Spartacus!"

The things I do for my readers!

## Amsterdam West

To do this part of Amsterdam justice, I will split it into two main neighborhoods: Oud West (Old West) and Bos en Lommer.

## Oud West

According to the teachings of the Roman Catholic church, Purgatory is the place between Heaven and Hell, where those who have not committed mortal sin are elected to go to Heaven. The same could be said of Oud West. Situated tantalisingly close to the Heaven of Amsterdam South and also within smartphone - snatching, easy scooter -riding distance to the Hell that is Bos en

Lommer.

If you want to see up and coming yuppies in their natural habitat, move to Oud West. This neighborhood is hip, consisting of Delicatessens, good wine dealers, and plenty of lively cafés. Back in the day, the Shallow Man could frequently be seen propping up the bar at café Oslo, fighting off the attentions of cheap-boot-wearing ladies with bad haircuts. Think of Manhattan's East Village and you'll be in the right ballpark. In recent years lots of renovations have taken place in the neighborhood, making it an incredibly good value place to buy or rent property. When visiting cafés for breakfast or lunch during the weekend, please be careful not to trip over and risk breaking your neck, due to selfish parents parking their bugaboo pushchairs anywhere they please. That aside, Amsterdam Oud West gets the Shallow Man's seal of approval, something I'm sure will bring joy to the hearts of members of the local council.

## Bos en Lommer

The Shallow Man, being the adventurous chap that he is, once visited a shortly-lived nightclub called The Moon. Unfortunately, like its name, it had absolutely no atmosphere. Which brings me to the part of Amsterdam West known as Bos en Lommer. If Dante were alive today, he'd have based his masterwork, Inferno, in Bos En Lommer. For those of you not familiar with Dante, he wrote about taking a tour through Hell. I'm sure that there's a Dante straat in Bos en Lommer somewhere. Like Amsterdam East, Bos en Lommer is at the very end of known civilisation. It's a long and perilous journey to get there, and upon arriving you'll soon realise that apart from the joys of doner (food, not a woman), some gambling halls and a few local social clubs, there is very little to do there.

The area is also well-known for its entrepreneurial spirit. Many small-business people have opened the largest collection of "Thuis bordeel's" (Home brothels) in the country. If you are looking for somewhere incredibly cheap to live, then this is the neighborhood for you. In fact, many properties there are so undesirable that landlords will practically pay you to move in.

If you are looking for a neighborhood where even taxi drivers are afraid to take passengers to (even though many of them live there) and want to be guaranteed a life of boredom and eternal torment, move to Bos en Lommer.

# BOOK 3, THE BOOK OF GLUTTONY

# JULY 11TH

My day started with a bit of a shock. While packing my Grey Worsted three-piece number and opting for a Navy Blue suit with razor-thin white piping, I received a call from the French Police. A Lieutenant Texier from the Paris Police wanted to meet me as soon as possible. I told him that he was in luck as I was planning to board the train to Paris in the next 40 minutes. He refused to discuss what he wanted to talk about over the phone, but said that it was a matter that was in both of our interests.

To say that I was in shock would have been an understatement. My encounters with the Police were far and few in between. To have to speak with a French policeman, I just didn't understand what he could possibly want from me. Well I was due to find out, he'd agreed that we could meet discreetly and informally in the Police Station closest to our offices in the La Defense area of Paris during my lunch break. With a sick feeling in the pit of my stomach, I took the train to Paris.

Koen, that overpaid son of a snake had opted to fly to Paris for the meeting as had our group marketing and communications specialist, Jessica, an irritating American forty something blonde who wore way too much makeup, but on the plus side was always smartly dressed.

The secondary purpose of today's meeting was to see the results of one of Christian's brainwaves, the customer centric service values program. This long collection of words, could only have been thought up by a German, used as they are to long convoluted sentences. The customer centric service values program, was Christian's response to criticism he'd received from his fellow partners, about the perceived lack of value provided by his business unit, International IT and Procurement.

Rather than addressing the actual problem, poor customer service, he instead dreamt up an internal marketing campaign, delivered by a firm of outrageously expensive, hair full of gel and white powder up the nose advertising types, to deliver an internal feel good promotional campaign, full of fluffy words and meaningless phrases. Koen, the expert in kissing Christian's sizeable butt, was almost on the verge of giving himself a heart attack, so enthusiastic was he over this venture. Ditto Jessica, who I'd known for several years, but to this day had yet heard her say anything that makes sense at all. Her main job was to degermanise Christian's tortured prose, turning it into meaningful English sentences.

The main purpose of the meeting in Paris was to sit through a presentation by our marketing gurus Spiggot, Lanson and Dirksen. A combination of British, French and Dutch marketing and design types with offices in Paris, London and Amstelveen.

As their office in Paris was so small as to make one claustrophobic, we opted to meet in our swankier and roomier premises in La Defence. From SLD, we were honoured to have one of the firms founding Partners, Charles Lanson, who had brought along Wela, a Dutch designer and Peter her copywriting partner.

Of course it wouldn't have been polite to ask Christian why Charles Lanson, the only person in the room to actually live in Paris, couldn't have met us all in Amsterdam. Far it be from me to ask obvious questions. At least Wela was easy on the eye. Early thirties, and pretty well dressed for a Dutch woman, in black trousers and a tight fitting matching top, that did a good job at presenting her perky breasts, which looked as if they'd had too much caffeine that morning.

Peter, was a typical Dutch giant, at least 186cm tall. His very appearance offended me. Bright red jeans, brown pointy shoes, a striped green shirt and a not too shabby smart tailored looking jacket. He was in serious need of a nose hair clipper.

Charles, was a fifty something silver fox. He was elegantly dressed in an exquisitely tailored grey striped three-piece suit. If I looked half as good at his age, I'd be a happy man. I liked Charles, there was a refreshing lack of bullshit about him, in-spite of his chosen profession.

The perky Wela then spoke up, and first recited the brief provided by Christian about making our customers feel that they are at the center of everything we do. (I'm trying not to laugh as I write this). She then did the incredibly daring and original thing of whipping out (not what I hoped sadly) white boards with the concepts mapped out. She and Peter the copywriter, then talked excitedly about how the campaign is a "game changer" and a paradigm shift in how the organization would view the services we provide.

Christian, Koen and Jessica lapped it up, like kittens with a bowl of milk. We sat there for two hours, with much excited squealing from Koen and grunting and enthusiastic noises from all present. My mind was elsewhere; I had a horrible sinking feeling and was dreading my encounter with the French Police. Once the meeting was over, and I'd said my goodbye to the silver fox and his minions, I made my excuses and headed for the meeting with Inspector Texier, a black Frenchman, who looked as if he spent far too much time in the gym.

His English was much better than I'd expected and he informed me that he wanted to talk to me as I was one of the last people to have seen Daniella Zadravec. Apparently, she hadn't been seen since the evening I'd been to dinner with her and Claudine. I assured the good Inspector that I couldn't remember much after leaving L'Avenue with her and Claudine, and that I had absolutely no recollection of where we'd gone or anything from that evening until I'd woken up in agony, throwing up in my hotel room.

He didn't appear to be in the least bit surprised by my story. He asked me a couple of questions about Claudine and gave me what he suggested was friendly advice, which was to steer well clear of her. When I asked him why, he refused to be drawn into any further discussion on the matter, and asked that we keep our conversation confidential. He told me that I might be hearing from him in the future, and then thanked me for taking the time to see him and that I was free to go. An unsettling experience.

I grabbed some food in our cafeteria, which in reality served better quality food than many of the so called Eetcafes I knew in Amsterdam. I then joined Christian and the team for a strategic meeting to discuss the thrilling subject of how we were going to roll out our customer-at –the-center-of-everything-we-do campaign to the rest of the organization. Some people are under the misconception that business trips are glamorous and fun; well, my day in Paris so far was living proof that the opposite was true.

Towards the end of another pointless day, I received a call from Claudine, who we were due to meet the following day in our office in Paris. "Simon, darling, how are you?" I was a bit alarmed to be receiving a call from her, so cautiously I responded,

"Claudine, I'm fine thanks, a bit busy actually,"

"Ok Simon, I won't keep you long, I was speaking to Charles Lanson earlier"

"you know Charles, silly question, of course you do"

"hahaha, I know everyone Simon, many more people than you think, anyway, Charles and I are going for dinner this evening at the Hotel Costes, and was wondering if you would like to join us."

I knew the Hotel Costes well, and had spent many an evening there propping up the bar and flirting with the ladies there. Following my previous encounter with Claudine, plus the warning from Inspector Texier, I should have steered well clear of Claudine, however, I had also eaten at the restaurant of the hotel, which was very good indeed.

"Ok Claudine, I'll join you for dinner, but nothing more, as I have to be up early for our meeting tomorrow"

"Of course Simon, just dinner, and by the way, it is on me, I insist"

"Thank you Claudine, much appreciated"

With that, we agreed to meet at the Hotel later that evening. I declined Christian's invitation to dinner with Koen and Jessica, hinting that I already had plans with a woman I knew in Paris, which in fact was the truth. Christian immediately took this as meaning something else, and with a touch of forced joviality said "oh you have a meeting with a woman you know here? You naughty boy, make sure she don't tire you out ja? You have work to do in the morning, and I want you here on time."

With that I left the office and after having checked in to my hotel in Etoile, jumped into a taxi and headed off to meet Claudine and Charles.

The Hotel Costes is situated in the Rue Saint Honorare, one of the most exclusive shopping streets in Paris. It makes the much hyped PC Hooftstraat (a favorite shopping place of mine in Amsterdam) look like a small provincial market street in comparison.

The boutique Hotel is a five star bastion of pure opulence and luxury, staffed by stunning looking women in designer clothes and beautiful designer stiletto shoes. Parked outside were the obligatory cars of the super rich, an Aston Martin here, a Ferrari there. I was ushered in past the security staff and welcomed by a red haired beauty, who with a lovely French accent, guided me on staggering high heels to an alcove in which Claudine was already seated with Charles, the silver fox.

As I approached, I could sense an atmosphere between them which immediately dissipated on my arrival, as Claudine rose to her feet and kissed me warmly on both cheeks. She was in a stunning white dress (Prada I later found out) with a super thin diamond watch on her wrist, and a pearl necklace and diamond earring combo which looked very fetching indeed. This was combined with matching white shoes, with black heels. She smelled like a fine perfumery, and in fact, I could only describe her entire appearance, from head to toe as being perfect.

Charles warmly shook my hand. A waitress, another beauty, poured me a glass of champagne from an already open bottle of

Krug Clos Du Mesnil. The face of the normally supremely composed silver fox, was a little red, which made me wonder how long they'd been sitting there drinking champagne.

"Simon, you did not enjoy today's meeting"

"Not at all Charles, I think you and your team delivered some outstanding work" I lied in response.

"Bullshit" he cried.

"Don't take me for a fool. I could see that you were not interested, and I agree with you that it was appalling work no? Twenty years ago we would have thrown Christian out into the street on his fat arsehole. Now we have to beg philistines like him for business.

"Calm down Charles" said Claudine in an amused tone.

"Be pleased that in these times of financial crisis, you still have clients silly enough to waste money this way, you agree Simon?"

"Yes, there's an old English saying, never look a gift horse in the mouth"

"Gift horse?, What is this gift horse? Why you talk about horses? I talk about fat, stupid, greedy Christian and his ego, this project is all about ego, but you Simon can see this, I saw the contempt in your eyes, you are wasted there"

"Now that, said Claudine, raising her champagne glass is something we can all agree on"

Charles, not to be put off his subject matter, continued "The stupid German cannot appreciate the work we could produce with the right brief, we throw him scraps and he laps it up like a hungry dog"

"Enough" hissed Claudine in a low but cutting tone that froze Charles and I in our tracks. There was something in the tone of her voice, a kind of threatening authority, a confidence, an implied threat that suddenly made me want to be anywhere but with the two of them at that moment. There was a strange dynamic between the two of them that became clearer during a fine meal of caviar, risotto with extra truffles, wagyu beef, foie gras, washed down with two bottles of 1986 Chateau Lafite Rothschild.

Following this incredible meal, we floated happily along to the Hotel Bar, one the best in Europe, if not the world. Beautiful mellow house music from the Hotel's own record label filled the bar, as did a collection of models, businessman, escort ladies and a few single older ladies. Just about everyone in the bar looked stunning. Having lived in Amsterdam for so long, the city that style forgot, being in a bar surrounded by beautiful and well dressed people I was like a tiger that had been held in a zoo, being returned to its natural habitat.

We took some seats at the bar that had just become vacant. Claudine ordered a 1988 Krug Champagne, against the wishes of Charles. They then had a brief but heated discussion in French with Claudine appearing to have the last word. She excused herself and left for the bathroom. Charles, shook his head. By now the silver fox was extremely red of face and unsteady on his feet.

"I should have known better than to ever have gotten involved with her," he said woefully.

"Involved? Are you two an item?"

"An item?" He laughed, "you mean a couple? Claudine, has no interest in my physical self, she only wants one thing from me"

"One thing? What's that then?" I asked intrigued.

"The one thing she cares about, if care is the correct word to use; Simon, don't mention our discussion to her, I beg you"

"What discussion?", I asked confused.

"We've not really had a discussion, plus, you haven't actually told me anything"

"Have I not?" said Charles, now leaning unsteadily against the bar.

"Good, that's very good"

At this point, Claudine suddenly appeared next to us. Our backs were seated facing away towards the bar, so we didn't see or hear her approach; it still freaked me out how she could just pop-up, like Marley's ghost (Jacob, not Bob) unseen and unheard.

I excused myself and paid a visit to what is probably one of the most sumptuous toilets I've ever had the pleasure of visiting. Situated in the basement of the Hotel, it's a marble beauty, clean, and fresh smelling. I rejoined Claudine, who was sat at the bar, sans Charles.

"What happened to Charles?" I asked

"He had a little too much to drink, and had to leave. It's a pity what he has become. He was such an inspiring man once and now…" she shook her head as she said this.

"He seems fine to me, and we have had a lot to drink" I said in defense of the silver fox.

"Fine? You think he's fine?" She repeated, her voice taking on a shrill tone.

"He's pathetic. A slave to his base needs and desires, his

addictions, petty hatreds, his vanity, and he's allowed it to bring him to his knees. No not his knees, his belly, yes his belly, like the serpent in the garden of Eden."

As she said this she broke into a hideous laugh that chilled the so called Shallow  Man to his box shorts.

"Simon, drink your champagne. I have plans for you this evening."

At that I glanced at my Rolex Submariner, and remembering the cryptic warning from Inspector Texier, began to make my excuses.

"Of course Simon, silly me, you're tired, you must have been awake very early to come to Paris today. Finish your champagne and I'll take you back to your hotel.

# JULY 12TH

It's 4.30 am and the first thing I can remember is that I'm wandering through the corridors of a hotel? My hotel? Yes it's my hotel. I'm naked apart from my Rolex, what is going on? Now what room was I staying in? Why can't I remember? Oh shit, someone's coming, it's a member of staff from the hotel.

"Can I help you sir?" His eyebrows are raised like Roger Moore as James Bond.

"Are you a guest at this hotel sir?"

"Yes, err look, I'm sorry, I must have gotten locked out of my room"

"Of course" he says, not bothering to suppress a laugh.

"Does sir have any ID with him?"

"ID? Yes, of course I do, it's stuffed up my arse"

"Really sir? Would you mind removing it and showing me?"

"Ok listen, my name is Simon Woolcot, I'm sure, or at least I hope that my ID is in the room."

At this, he got on a radio and began speaking rapidly in French.

"You are in room 605, come with me sir"

I followed him to my room, which he then opened. Luckily, my clothes were strewn all over the room. My beautiful suit, jacket on the floor, trousers on the bed, shirt in the bathroom. What the fuck is going on? I quickly put on my Armani boxer shorts. I managed to find my ID in the inside pocket of my suit jacket, which was verified by the grinning security card. I apologized to him for the bother.

"Don't worry Mr Woolcot, I've seen much worse, I suggest that you lock the door from the inside to prevent you from sleepwalking.".

He winked as he said this, and I gave him a 20 euro tip, (luckily the wallet was there and intact) to send him on his way, with a grateful shake of the hand.

I had a restless sleep. Wandering around naked in the corridor had certainly sobered me up. I wasn't as bad as the last time I'd been in Paris, but had a restless sleep full of strange dreams. I was in a hot place, a dungeon. Claudine was there, dressed in outrageous rubber or leather underwear, and this time in incredibly high heels. There were other people present in masks. I was sure that I heard the voice of Charles, moaning and weeping. I could hear Claudine's voice tormenting him, "you can look but you can't touch", "you're a loser, a failure, a result of your own desires," followed by much laughter of those present.

I lay prostrate, naked on a table to which I was bound, with belts all over my body, on my back. Loud music played in the background, it was hot and I remember being surrounded by a mixture of people in various states of undress and stroked, caressed, kissed and then the hotel.

Fearful of being late again for a meeting with Christian, I'd arranged for an early morning call as well as the alarm on my phone ringing at 8am, but was awoken by knocking on the door of my hotel room by a serious and imposing looking Inspector Texier from the French Police. I let him in. Taking a seat after removing my discarded clothes and placing them on the bed he exclaimed:

"So Mr. Woolcot, you don't believe in following the friendly advice of Policemen"

"If Inspector, you're referring to associating with Claudine, well things kind of happened and just got a little out of hand" I interrupted him before he could continue.

"I gave you good advice, which you ignored, do you even remember what happened last night?" He asked, his eyes never leaving mine for a second.

"I don't remember much after we left Hotel Costes" I admitted, embarrassed.

"Did you at any time leave your glass unattended while you were with Claudine and her companion?"

"Well Inspector, we had a lot to drink and obviously I had to visit the toilet a couple of times."

"So Mr Woolcot", he said triumphantly, like a woman who has just proved that her suspicions about a cheating spouse were proved right.

"Less than 24 hours ago, I advised you to steer clear of Claudine, instead of which you went and did exactly the opposite".

"Well yes Inspector but,"

"DON'T INTERRUPT ME WHEN I'M TALKING TO YOU." shouted a clearly annoyed Inspector Texier.

"Luckily for you, I had a man follow you yesterday. He was in the Hotel bar the entire evening, and followed you and Claudine on to the establishment you visited afterwards." Trying to explain my point, I cautiously asked him if I could speak, then pointed out the following.

"I met Claudine for dinner, only because I knew that Charles was going to be there as well. My plan was to leave immediately after dinner, but then we had a drink in the bar, and I really was planning to go after a polite drink but"

"But," replied the Inspector.

"She drugged your champagne"

"She did what?" I asked, unbelievingly.

"How naive are you Simon? You don't object to me calling you Simon? No, ok, listen. How naive do you have to be to ignore the warning of a policeman and ignore your own instincts. This is not the first time that something unusual has occurred after an evening out with Claudine, am I right? I know that I am right as the night Daniela was last seen, the three of you were together. My information is that the next morning you were heard being sick. I know you have nothing to do with her sudden disappearance as the last person to be seen with her, leaving your hotel room very much alive was Claudine."

I was shocked by this and it obviously showed on my face. The Inspector, now spoke softly as he asked,

"Have you ever heard of Gamma-Hydroxybutyrate?" Also more commonly known as GHB?"

I had dabbled in marijuana from time to time, but hard drugs were completely outside of my terms of reference. I informed him of this.

"GHB is known as the date rape drug. It can be administered in a liquid form, and is odorless and tasteless, making it the perfect drug to mix with alcohol, for example champagne."

I was completely confused.

"Date rape drug?" I asked, "I don't need any kind of drug to have sex with Claudine, have you seen her?"

The Inspectors face took on an angry expression as moving closer to me he said,

"Stop thinking in such narrow terms. Did you not notice certain side effects? Increased sex drive, memory loss, nausea, possible vomiting, does this sound familiar to you?"

Suddenly, things were becoming clearer; so that was the reason for me feeling like death last time.

"But why would she drug me? I'd have jumped into bed with her in a minute".

"Claudine wouldn't have drugged you to have sex with you; she'd have had other motives. As you are not married, even though you are in your mid forties, blackmail can't have been the reason. Yet she never does anything without a reason, and I am sure the reason for her doing so will reveal itself to you soon".

Stunned, I asked him why the Police were following her; she was after all, an account director in a major telecoms organization.

Clearly irritated, and with a touch of sarcasm he retorted,

"So you think we are stupid? You think the French Police has nothing better to do with public money than to harass innocent businesswomen?

"No, I didn't say that Inspector"

"You didn't say this, but it was implied in the question. Claudine, is a person of interest, and not the kind of woman an oversexed Englishman should spend time with." I was going to respond with a joke that there was no such thing as oversexed but thought better of it.

"If you must spend time with her, in the future, you must keep your eyes on your drink at all times, do not let it out of your sight. My officer followed you to an exclusive, how you say, underground club, last night, but was unable to get in as it is invitation only. He witnessed you leaving that club half dressed and not in a good mental state several hours later. He took you back to your hotel, but omitted to lock the door of your room, which is why you were wandering the corridors naked in the early hours of the morning."

Not remembering much of this, I could only hold my head in my hands with shame.

"Not remembering, is a side effect of the drug, one that Claudine is relying on. She obviously used a smaller dosage this time, as you have recovered pretty quickly and I assume can remember some details?"

"Some, but not much. Some kind of dungeon, being tied up, not much more really"

He reached for his wallet and handed me a card.

"When you are back in Amsterdam, you will hear from Claudine again. If you do, and you receive an invitation to a party known as the 'Love Palace' you are to contact my colleague in the Amsterdam Police, Brigadier Woudstra."

I tried pressing him for more information on what was going on, but he insisted that the less I knew the better. He wished me a good trip back to Amsterdam, then left. I hurried to our office in Paris and sat through a morning of tedium, repetition and bore witness to Olympic quality arse kissing by Koen and Jessica. Following an unremarkable lunch for which I had no appetite, I left and took the Thalys back to the friendlier climes of Amsterdam, or so I thought.

Arrived early Friday afternoon back at the Woolcot palace. Took a normal taxi from Central Station back home. Big mistake, as I immediately had to listen to a taxi driver whining about the fact that he was finding it hard to make a living. What he really meant was that the days of charging clueless tourists and anyone that spoke English double the normal rate were now over, due to Amsterdam council finally brining in laws with punitive fines for drivers caught ripping off passengers.

As if I didn't have enough problems of my own. I ignored the ranting of the taxi driver and attempted to focus on my own issues. Claudine, GHB, Daniela missing, all far too much for a shallow man to deal with. I decided to call Anna, and arranged to meet her for dinner later that evening. What she'd make of the mess I'd got myself into was anyone's guess.

# TIPS FOR NAVIGATING THE AMSTERDAM TAXI WAR ZONE

One of the reasons that I never became a journalist apart from the fact that I can't spell, and have suspect grammar is because I was terrified that I might have ended up being sent to some terrible part of the world in the middle of a war zone. So the Shallow Man took a different, safer path until I ended up moving to the fair and pleasant place known as Amsterdam.

I've been to many cities across Europe and the rest of the world and yet, I must say that Amsterdam has the worst and most dishonest taxi drivers I've ever had the misfortune of dealing with.

When I first moved here, after a night of partying at Palladium (dodging the Gol Diggers) and at Jimmy Woo, where I'd had a Vodka Orange or four or five, I decided that as it was the middle of winter, instead of walking for 15 to 20 minutes home, I'd take a taxi.

So I walked up to the Leidseplein taxi rank which had a huge line of taxis lined up, so far so good; however, there were hordes of people hanging around. As I reached the taxi rank you could cut the atmosphere there with a Chainsaw. Tension was in the air, aggressive drivers were arguing with potential passengers as if it were a Moroccan Bazaar.

I approached what I assumed to be an available car. "I'd like to go to the Sarphartipark," I asked politely. "Where? Sarphartipark? Ok get in," replied the driver who'd obviously recently graduated from charm school. As soon as the cab pulled away from Leidseplein, the driver shut off the meter, turned to me and said "Sarphartipark that be 25 Euros." Trying not to laugh I responded "I'll pay the price that's on the meter and not a euro cent more, so the first thing I suggest that you do is turn the meter back on." The driver shook his head, "No, no, no man, you pay 25 Euros, no meter." Unfortunately for the driver, who'd obviously assumed that being an English speaker, I was some dumb tourist, I actually knew a little about the Amsterdam taxi laws so was able to tell him that the law requires that all journeys in a taxi are compliant to the agreed tariff per KM, per minute and must be measured on the meter which must be turned on.

"If you don't turn the meter on I'll simply take a photo of your license plate and will report you on the Taxiklacht.nl website." Upon hearing this his entire demeanor changed, he indeed turned on the meter and for the rest of the short journey cursed under his breath in a language I could not comprehend. Upon arriving I paid him the exact amount that was on the meter and took my time about finding the money just to annoy him even further.

I've had several such experiences with Amsterdam taxi drivers. Since June 1st the city council have brought in a new law which is intended to make sure that taxi drivers are easily identifiable, with the number of the driver in plain sight on the roof of the car. One of the big problems with the taxi market in Amsterdam was that many cowboy drivers would come into town from all over the country during the weekends with the sole aim of ripping off tourists. Now it's only possible to pick up passengers from taxi ranks or the street if the driver is in possession of an Amsterdam Council permit. If a driver is caught working in Amsterdam without a permit, or behaves as I outlined above, they can be fined up to 20,000 Euros.

# BOOK 4, THE BOOK OF ENVY

# JULY 13TH

My Friday evening was not what I expected. I'd arranged to meet Anna, expecting to have some tea and sympathy from my old friend. We met at Gambrinus for dinner, a super little Eetcafe in our Amsterdam neighborhood.

Over some delicious fish and a glass of wine, I told her the sorry tale of Daniela's disappearance, my encounter with Inspector Texier and the blackout and my eventual wandering naked through the corridor of the hotel.

She listened attentively, and impassively. I would have hated to have played poker with her. Well strip poker perhaps, anyway, she listened and then blew her top.

"You'll never learn will you Simon? All of this is your own fault." Outraged, I asked her to justify her statement. "So Anna, you're telling me that just for being the sociable chap that I am, that I deserve to be drugged, have God knows what done to me and then be dragged into the middle of a Police investigation? I'm really not following your reasoning here."

This seemed only to put oil on the fire, as she then spoke through gritted teeth in a tone that told me she was only a step away from hitting me.

"This is your fault and you just don't see it. Actually Simon, you don't see anything, even if it's right under your nose, mein Gott, you really are *the* shallow man. The reason you're in this situation is because of greed, no not greed," she then said a word in German that translated to gluttony.

"Yes Simon you're a glutton. You have to consume and you never get enough. I was hoping that by taking the time out of your pointless life to write a diary that it would help you to reflect. That it would hold up a mirror to you on your life and where you're going wrong."

I was getting irritated now, who was she to start lecturing me?

But she wouldn't let me interrupt, and continued in the same vein.

"You have so much Simon and yet none of it means anything to you. We are all disposable to you. Life is just a game. You move on from woman to woman to restaurant to bar, to party, nothing changes in your life, only the women. You're over 40, you can't keep living like this."

Nothing in the statement she made seemed wrong to me, I suppressed a smile and answered her criticisms head on.

"I thought that you and I are supposed to be good friends?

"We are friends Simon, but I'm worried about you, don't you

see that?" Her tone had softened.

"There's nothing to worry about Anna, I'm fine".

"Simon, being drugged by a strange woman and having the Police involved is not my definition of fine".

Damn, I had to give her that one.

"Simon, I always hoped you'd change, or grow out of what I thought was a phase you were going through after you split up with Lucy. But now, I'm really worried. Your relationship with women is a big problem in your life, can't you see that?

I decided honesty was called for and told her that actually there are many terms that could be used to describe my interactions with the opposite sex, but problems wouldn't be a description I'd use.

"Simon, you fuck different women, maybe you think you're using them, actually, you don't think you're using them, you just consume, blindly. You go from woman to woman, there's no love there, can you remember what it was like to be in love Simon? Not lust, but love, not fucking, but making love, do you remember?

She hit a nerve there. Love, was like the song that you used to enjoy in the distant past but couldn't quite remember what it was called anymore, or even how it went. My heart actually skipped a beat as my mind wandered back to… no stop it. Got to get this under control, this is not me.

"Listen Anna, I respect you, and I enjoy your company but I really don't want to hear it. You're overreacting. I went out with a supplier a couple of times and it turns out that she's a mad date rape drug doping bitch who's in trouble with the cops. It could have happened to anyone". At this point she interrupted and shouted,

"It couldn't have happened to anyone but you, because you can't get enough!" With that she told me that she'd had enough of me for one evening, left her dinner uneaten and went home.

A wiser man would have gone home and reflected on the conservation with Anna. Instead I stayed on in the bar and had several glasses of Sauvignon Blanc. Even spoke with a couple of loud, jean wearing Dutch ladies with bad hair, before deciding to head home.

I called Irina, and did something I would normally never do, I invited her round to the Woolcot palace. I'm not a great fan of having women round for the night. The Shallow Man is an island whose borders are almost permanently closed. Superman had his fortress of solitude, I have my palace of entertainment. My apartment is not female friendly and that's how I like it. No plants, paintings, pictures of family members, former pets, or any fluffy stuff. Just 110 square meters of cold functional state of the art home entertainment system that set me back almost 10,000 Euros. The sound quality is so good that I'm quite happy locking myself away for hours on the PlayStation or listening to John Coltrane or Radiohead. A leather sofa, beautiful coffee table, a designer kitchen, built in wardrobes and a well used king sized bed. All paid for by the good chaps and chapesses who mâkeup the Partnership of Mcculloch.

Irina came round. I didn't share details of my adventures in Paris with her and after some obligatory small talk we ended up having a hot night of passion.

It was the first time that she'd spent the night at my place. Normally I send her home in a taxi or generally avoid having her come to my place if I can help it, but I was still a little unsteady following the previous night's events and felt like some human company to wake up next to.

I woke up late in the morning to strange noises coming from a room in the apartment that I rarely use, the kitchen. Irina was already awake and fully dressed, making breakfast. I knew that my designer kitchen cupboards were usually empty, so she must have gone out and bought some food while I was asleep.

"Thanks Irina, how much did you spend on food? Shall I give you some money?" I asked.

"No need, I took some out of wallet" of course what else, I thought. Irina is like the British monarchy, she firmly believes in never carrying any form of cash with her at all, at least when she's in my company. I decided not to tell her off for helping herself to money in my wallet. I'm sure I had over 150 Euros cash, but upon checking saw that there was only 50 left.

"Bloody hell Irina, what did you buy for breakfast? Lobsters and Caviar?" Big mistake. She was facing away from me preparing some scrambled eggs at the stove, in a pair of leggings that were criminally tight. She turned to me, suddenly red faced and screamed,

"How dare you? What you accuse me of? You think I steal money from you? I get out of bed, go to market, bought you food not only for breakfast, but for dinner tonight as I cook for you". Alarm bells rang at the mention of dinner, I had no plans to keep her around that long.

"You think I am bitch no?" She was really shouting now.

"Irina, calm down, I simply asked you a question, and the usual response to a question is to politely answer and not hit the bloody roof. I'm grateful to you for going shopping, it's not often that I have a hot women in my kitchen making me breakfast." With this I threw my arms around and her and hugged her tightly. At first she held her body tense and stiff, but soon relented and hugged me back. We kissed and then removing her blouse, she said

"So you like a hot woman cooking for you in the kitchen? How you like this?" She said in a playful tone and stripped down to her skimpy underwear.

"Irina, call me shallow, but I like, very much" I said imitating her Russian accent.

Following a delicious breakfast of scrambled eggs with goats cheese and mushrooms, we made good use of the Shallow Man's leather sofa for an hour and then satiated, fell asleep in each others arms on the sofa while listening to the music of John Coltrane and Miles Davis.

We were awoken by an alert message from my iPhone. There were actually several messages. Irina eyed me carefully as I read them:

Message from Richard:
Oi Woolcot, sorry for the low profile lately. Let's meet up, I've got something to show you.

Message from Leonie:
Hi Simon, I've not heard from you for awhile, are you free on Monday for a drink?

Message from Anna:
Hi Shallow Man. Sorry for losing my temper with you last night, I'm just really worried about you. You're like the farmer that goes out and buys canned meat every day and yet he has so much quality meat to choose from right in front of him on his farm. ☺ ☺

Anna's message was way too cryptic for me. Farms, tinned meat? That's German humor for you. I responded to Anna's message.
"Ich verstehe dich ueberhaupt nicht (I don't understand you at all)
Irina, much to my displeasure, leaned over to me and tried to look at what I was typing and to who.

"Irina, do you mind? I don't like people looking over my shoulder when I'm reading."
"Have something to hide do you Simon?"
Trying to hide my irritation at having her still present on my island and sticking her Russian nose in my business,
"Show me a man over the age of forty that has nothing to hide and I'll show you a corpse in a mortuary."
With that I rose and walked into the spare room to continue reading and responding to my messages in private.

From Simon to Leonie
"Hi Leonie, Monday is good 4 me. Let's meet at the Tunes Bar in the Conservatorium Hotel at 8."

From Simon to Richard
"The ghost of King Richard walks the Earth. Finally. I have Irina round at the moment. Will kick her out, come round in an hour for a PS3 session."

From Richard to Simon
"No problem, prepare to lose. I'll see if Nat can get away from the wife as well.

I dispatched Irina, with much whaling and gnashing of teeth. "Why I can't stay and watch you play computer games?" I explained to her that gaming with ones friends was one of the all male pastimes and that I wouldn't be like John Lennon, who was the first Beatle to break the golden rule of not having women in the studio.
"My name isn't John and you're certainly no Yoko, so please respect our tradition and I'll see you later for dinner."
She then attempted to unzip my pants, but I knew her tricks and with a huff, she flounced out of my apartment.

I spent some time updating the diary with the previous nights events and then the buzzer rang and for the first time in some time, I met Richard.

He certainly looked different from his normal self. Usually, he dressed in what I'd describe as a slightly haphazard fashion, with clothes just randomly thrown together with little thought for things like coordination, but today he was looking incredibly dapper. He was wearing a pair of quality black jeans, (Armani I later confirmed) and a pair of boots from my favorite shoe wear firm, Church. He had a Versace silk black shirt and was wearing an expensive looking wafer thin leather jacket, that was silk smooth to the touch.

"What the hell has happened to you? Did you win the lottery? I asked, totally taken aback by his change of appearance.

"Check out the watch, Simon" he said pointing to the object of my desires, a Gold Hublot watch. A feeling of rage, jealousy and hatred suddenly rose within me. I quickly swallowed the feelings down and demanded that he tell me how in the name of Bob Marley he could afford the watch.

"Well Simon, I told you that I did a deal with the Devil, and I can only tell you that Satan pays very well. I can put in a word if you like. The Devil's work is never done."

I was just about to ask him to explain what he meant, who he was working for and more importantly what work he could possibly be doing that pays obviously more than his full-time job, when the door buzzed again and I let in Nat, the most pussy-whipped man on the planet.

I opened some beers that I keep in the fridge for my primitive friends and in spite of an attempted Guantanamo bay style interrogation of Richard by both Nat and me, he refused to tell us anything about his work with the Devil. We gave up and moved on to the more substantive matter of playing Pro-evolution Soccer, followed by Call of Duty.

While playing, Richard, concentrating heavily on not being beaten by Nat in Call of Duty, asked me,

"So who are you shagging at the moment? You still porking that Russian girl?" Nat, suddenly turned his attention away from the screen.

"Yeah Simon, come on, who's the latest in the Woolcot collection? What was her name? Irina right?"

Being the well raised gentleman that I am, I simply acknowledged her continued role in my recreational activities without saying anything further. Nat, pressed on.

"Russian girls are supposed to be great in bed. I know they're your weakness."

"No comment," I replied, tight lipped.

"Come on man, you know I'm married, I have to live vicariously through my friends. Especially with your track record. Come on Simon, don't be a poof, share some details." Nat was practically foaming at the mouth as he said this. I refused to discuss the subject any more, in spite of further questions from Richard, such as.

"So does she take it up Hershey highway? Or is she Russian

orthodox?" Such is the level of conversation when I get together with my friends, and Anna calls *me* shallow.

We played and time passed quickly as the door to my apartment opened and letting herself in, with a key to the Woolcot palace was Irina.

Nat and Richard gave each other shocked glances. I was also taken aback by the fact that she had made a copy of my keys, as the original set were lying in plain sight on the coffee table.

I introduced Irina to Nat and Richard, something I never wanted to do, as I do like to keep my friends and lovers in separate compartments, but well she'd already met Anna I suppose.

"Nice to meet you finally," Irina said to Richard, who was reaching for his beautiful leather jacket that he'd hung on the back of a chair. Nat also got ready to leave. His wife had already texted him and called him and he'd only stayed with us to avoid the abuse which he knew would follow him if he'd left the moment she'd called. Relieved to have a reason to leave my place, Nat scurried off back to his demanding better half. I walked with Richard down to the street and with serious concern asked him to tell me what was going on in his life.

"Nothing is going on mate, I'm good, better than good, I'm rolling in it. As I told you, the Devil pays good money. We'll catch up another time, you know what? I'll even take you to one of your fancy restaurants and pick up the tab, how about that?"

We agreed to call and make arrangements later. When I returned to the apartment, Irina, had already stripped down to her underwear and high heels.

"Your friends are nice, I like them. I go cook for you now. Relax, play your computer game if you like.

"Console game, not computer game." I corrected her.

"Whatever, play your little boy games and mummy will cook you a nice meal."

Another thing that hadn't gone unnoticed by me was that she'd arrived with several bags. I didn't like the look of this, but know that women like Irina, always like to have several outfits available in case something comes up.

She cooked a terrific moussaka, with a delicious salad that we accompanied with a bottle of Chateau Margeaux from 2005. Over dinner we discussed our previous encounter with Natasha and the, for me unseen, but well and truly heard Dmitry. Who I definitely didn't like the sound of.

"Natasha should have warned us about him. He is dangerous

man. You don't want to get involved with him, he is Devil." That caught my attention.

"Do they call Dmitry the Devil?" I asked, wondering how on earth Richard could be involved with him.

"I did not say he was the Devil, I said he is a Devil."

"Stay away from Natasha, if you involve with her, the Devil is bound to follow."

# THE SHALLOW MAN'S GUIDE TO AMSTERDAM IJBURG

The Shallow Man, recalls a tale he was once told. The story of the richest man in the world, who was so wealthy he could afford to have his whims, fancies and heart's desires fulfilled with a snap of his diamond covered fingers. However, there was one thing that eluded him. The secret of eternal life. This he sought above all else, as he reasoned, what was the point in being so rich and yet die eventually like some common pauper.

To this end, he sent out a team of experts to scour the world for a formula that would provide him with eternal life. Eventually, after many years of searching, his team found a remote and uncharted island on which they were told lived a tribe that had the secret of eternity. Excited he made the long and perilous journey to the island, along with plenty of gold, the price the tribe demanded for sharing their secret.

The gold was taken by the tribe and the wealthy man drank a cup of an elixir which would grant him eternal life. Upon drinking, he fell into a deep sleep, and when he awoke he was surprised to see that he was sat on a stool in a cage, made of gold. He attempted to rise from the stool but was completely unable to move a muscle, nor was he able to speak. He sat and is still sitting there frozen for eternity in a golden cage, on an island called Ijburg, which brings me to the subject of today's post.

The Shallow Man, in his continuing series on the various neighborhoods of Amsterdam has braved angry comments from the residents of each area he has covered so far, to bring the truth about various parts of the city to his public. Yet again, I will risk life, limb and exquisitely tailored three-piece suits, to bring the good news unto my flock. The things I do for my readers!

Ijburg, spans six artificial islands in Amsterdam East. I've previously described the East part of the city as being depressing and difficult to get to, well all of this and more applies to the "mistakes on the lake" that make up Ijburg.

Being artificial and relatively new, the area consists of many beautiful, newly built apartment complexes, developed to a standard rarely seen in Amsterdam.

The apartments often come with underground car parking for residents, private gyms, swimming pools and entertainment facilities. Something which is quite common in condominiums in Toronto or New York.

The Shallow Man knows people who live in Ijburg, and they

have beautiful apartments, but unfortunately, nothing else. The geniuses that developed the area, only created a single main road/bridge that connects it with Amsterdam, so it is not uncommon to see traffic jams in the morning of people attempting to leave the neighbourhood.

Unlike many other parts of Amsterdam, Ijburg lacks the vibrant bar, Eetcafe and restaurant scene which is commonplace in most parts of the city. When in Ijburg, one can't help but feel as if you are wandering around a giant film set, so bereft is it of people or atmosphere.

"Yes but look at the quality of the apartments, they're fantastic", is the common response from the residents of Ijburg, and yes it's a wonderful place to be if you choose never to leave your apartment.

Prior to the recession, much property development took place there, which has led to many now standing empty and available at competitive prices.

Nothing of any interest ever happens there. If you are planning to visit people that live there, arrive 30 minutes early, as the hunt for a suitable parking place can take some considerable time.

It's so quiet there that during a cold winter a man slipped in his brown shoes on ice and lay frozen and undiscovered for several days.

There is a single solitary tram that goes to Ijburg, or as it's better known, the island of the isolated.

Visit this island and you'll find people, in their lovely apartments, frozen for all eternity, trapped, knowing that it's simply too much trouble to go anywhere else in Amsterdam and too plain tedious to step outside of their houses.

It's the only place in Amsterdam that I'll not give taxi drivers a hard time for not knowing how to find places on the island; after all, only a hardcore group of the damned live there, and are rarely visited.

If you are looking to live in a luxurious newly built property, then this is definitely the place for you. However, do be prepared to spend up to 30 to 40 minutes to get to civilisation and be prepared for the excuses of friends who'll suddenly have last minute emergencies or other plans when they are scheduled to visit you. Other than that, it's a nice place to live.

# JULY 14TH

Irina stayed the night at my place. I must admit to quite enjoying having her around, and not only for wild and uninhibited sex. It's nice sometimes to wake up next to someone and to go to sleep with a warm body in my arms. I'd have to snap out of whatever was happening with me.

This was precisely why it was a bad idea to allow women onto one's island. Once they are on, they have a habit of clinging like plaque and twice as difficult to remove. I had to start formulating an exit plan to get rid of her.

Following another exceptional breakfast, this time of poached eggs, with some Parma ham that she'd bought with my money the day before, came a session with her on her knees worshiping the Woolcot physique. I showered and then went for a 20 kilometer run.

On my return, I was not happy to see that she'd obviously made an attempt to access my iPhone. Fortunately, at Mcculloch, we had a policy of protecting all smartphones with a six digit pin number. She'd obviously tried any number of combinations and hadn't realized that this in turn would completely wipe my phone after four failed attempts.

"What the hell were you doing trying to access my phone?" I asked her angrily.

"I just wanted to take a look, I only have an old phone, so I was just curious." She responded in a little sweet girly voice.

"Bollocks!"

"Do you really think that I'm going to buy that bullshit answer Irina? You were trying to read my texts and email. This is precisely why I don't normally allow women to stay at my place. Exactly to avoid this kind of scenario."

"Are you going to throw me out?" Her voice suddenly went adult again.

"I bloody well should".

She walked off in the direction of my walk-in wardrobe and returned with a belt with which she wound both hands together.

"I understand honey, I've been a bad girl, why you don't punish me?"

Needless to say, that being the shallow man that I am, I indeed did punish her and allowed her to stay on.

# THE SHALLOW MAN'S GUIDE TO EXPAT EVENTS

Over the years, the Shallow Man has found a common occurrence, the habit of people of varying nationalities, while living in a foreign land to huddle together as if they are the last surviving members of their race. People that would rarely mix socially in their home countries, suddenly cling to each other like the survivors of a shipwreck on a raft, which brings me to the subject of today's post, Expat organisations in the Netherlands.

The Shallow Man, during his nine year stint as an Expat in the Netherlands, has attended many events, organised by various organisations, all with a single aim in mind, to get their share of the Expat Euro. The Shallow Man will provide tips on how to cope with these organisations and their grasping, no sorry, helpful, only in it to enrich your miserable life, organizers. I do so at some considerable risk to my beautifully dressed self, but nevertheless will speak the truth about Expat organisations, even if it means being rounded up by a posse of event organizers and forced onto a Ryan Air flight back to London. The things I do for my readers!

Have you ever seen the excitement of a cat when it corners a mouse? Or a lion when chasing a pack of antelopes, and the youngest and most inexperienced one is left at its mercy? Join an Expat organisation, attend an event, and let the organizer know that you are a new member. You'll witness what Tex Avery, one of the creators behind the Looney Tunes cartoon franchise, used to show as Tweety pie, appearing in the eyes of Sylvester as a roasted chicken.

Some event organisers view Expats as being a bag of cash with legs and a mouth.

The Shallow Man has attended many Expat events over the years. Here is my guide to coping with them.

## Exclusive expat organizations

Be wary of organizations that claim to be incredibly exclusive, for example, membership is by invitation only. Some of these groups, work on the premise that being invitation only makes them more exclusive than other open ones. However, if you dig beneath the surface you'll find that, in the absence of an invitation, it's quite simple to join such a group, just by filling out a simple statement, explaining what makes you an international man or woman of mystery. Several lines of BS, a click and voila, you are now a member of an 'exclusive' Expat group.

Once you are a member of the exclusive group, you'll find that to use anything but the most basic functionality of the site will require you to pay a subscription fee.

## Open organizations

The so called 'Open' organizations, in other words, free ones, are generally run by a collection of sharks, who will arrange an event at a location that normally doesn't charge an entry fee. The event will be advertised as an exclusive party, for members of the open group only and will cost, for example, 10 euros a ticket. So far so good. What becomes clear later is that other members of the public, i.e. non-expats, can wander into the party and pay no entry fee. The organisers obviously expect that, as Expats are a species from another planet, under no circumstances will they speak with anyone who isn't an expat. The money grabbing organisers, who do a poor job at faking chumminess and joviality, go home several hundred euros richer as a result of the naivety of people with more money than sense.

# JULY 15$^{TH}$

Left for work the next morning following a screaming argument with Irina. To be fair, she was doing most of the screaming. This is not how I like to start my day, especially on a Monday morning. After letting her rant on, sometimes in English, other times in Russian, I finally lost my patience and threw her out of my apartment. She'd already moved far too many clothes into my walk-in wardrobe, plus had started filling up my bathroom cabinets with all manner of female hair and beauty products. The argument was my opportunity to get her off my island once and for all. I grabbed the opportunity with both hands, helped her pack and ordered an estate car taxi to take her back to her pokey little apartment. Free at last!

The cause of our argument, was my blatant honesty with Irina that I'd made arrangements to meet a stripper called Leonie for a drink. She'd asked me if I planned to fuck her. "Well Irina, we probably won't have penetrative sex, but she did promise me a free sample of her breasts, which I must admit, did look quite spectacular." This set Irina off in a rage. Very strange considering some of the games we've played in the past, including with the hot, but Dmitry owned, Natasha.

As we'd started arguing pretty early in the day, I managed to arrive at work earlier than usual. As my driver pulled in front of the building, who did I see pulling into our car park but the snake Koen, driving a brand spanking new BMW five series. Was he doing this deliberately to annoy me? Unbelievable.

With a broad smile I approached him.

"Nice car Koen. Bit of a change from the what was it a Volvo?" Beaming with pride, as indeed he should have been, Koen then spent the next minutes extolling the virtues of his new car, giving me a blow by blow explanation of every single feature. I had to admit that it was a beautiful car, with more gadgets than a dominatrix. As I said this to him, I suddenly had a sharp flashback to my night in a hot dungeon in Paris. Did Claudine, really do what I was starting to remember? Or was it just a dirty fantasy of mine?

Koen and I walked into the office with him still rabbiting on about his precious car. He's become very full of himself lately. If ever there was a man that needed taking down a peg or two and shown the importance of stoic humility, he was definitely the one. An evil plan began to form in my head.

As well as my planned assignation with the hot Leonie, I'd also been receiving messages from my poisonous ex-girlfriend

Lucy via stalkbook, sorry Facebook.

From Lucy to Simon:
"So I see that nothing changes with you. I've been watching the number of female friends that you have. Who's Leonie? She looks like a fucking whore. Jessica, don't like the look of her either. So you are into creative types now are you? Hope she's original in the bedroom.

From Lucy to Simon:
Don't ignore me you piece of shit. How dare you? I told you that'll be in Amsterdam soon. The dates are confirmed and whether you choose to ignore me or not, I will see you Simon Woolcot!

I, of course, did the only thing that was called for under the circumstances, I ignored her messages. That evening, after several stops, starts and false alarms, managed to confirm with Leonie and her friend Patrycja, who also kindly became a friend on Facebook, our meeting for a drink at 7.30 that evening.

After a day of listening to Koen, explain to everyone in minute detail the joys of his new car, I was in need of a drink or five.

I hadn't heard anything from the Inspector, which was a relief. Every time my phone rang I jumped out of my skin, expecting to hear from him. Luckily, so far so good, hadn't heard a thing.

Following a quick meal of Thai fried rice with vegetables, from my favorite Thai place in the Pijp, I had a quick shower, then changed into a pair of Karl Lagerfeld black jeans, a Versace silk shirt and a light cream leather jacket from Hugo Boss. These were worn with a pair of Boots from Church menswear.

It was a beautiful evening as I walked to the Conservatorium Hotel, past MuseumPlein, where hordes of tourists were milling around, taking photos of themselves in front of the I am Amsterdam sign, so that they could shock friends and relatives back home with cries of, "Guess where I was on holiday? Yes, Amsterdam, here's the proof."

I arrived at the Conservatorium Hotel, so called as the building where it's housed used to be music school. Now, beautifully renovated, airy, light and elegant, and home to a five star boutique Hotel, I felt perfectly at home there.

As I arrived at the cocktail bar, Leonie and Patrycja, were

already there, sat at the bar, receiving lots of attention from the other patrons of the establishment. Leonie was wearing skin tight leather trousers with high heeled shoes. She wore a loose fitting top, which her sizeable breasts were doing their best to escape from, much to the joy of a couple of suited Dutch estate agent types with slicked back Lion King like hair and brown shoes. Patrycia, was equally attention grabbing in a mini skirt that could have passed as a belt. Knee high leather boots, and a virtually see-through short sleeved cream top. While her breasts were not as impressive as Leonie's, they were pretty much visible, as were her tattoos that looked none too attractive.

"Simon, how are you?" said Leonie, giving me her hand and then leaning in for the typical Dutch tradition three kisses on the cheek.

"You remember Patrycia?" I couldn't really say that I did, but I nodded politely and as I was leaning forward to greet her with the three kisses greeting, grabbed my butt, then turning to Leonie said "You were right, he has a good arse."

With this, both girls screeched with laughter.

"What are you drinking ladies?" I asked, with the term lady used somewhat optimistically in their case.

"We've already ordered Long Island Ice Teas." A cocktail I swore long ago to stay away from as it absolutely had a habit of blowing my head off. I ordered a Mojito and then sat on a stool next to them, much to the disappointment of the estate agent types who were hovering around, like sharks at an Australian harbour.

"So Leonie, as I was saying" said Patrycia in an ear aching tone, with a strong Polish accent,

"If you want to put your thing in that hole, it will cost you another 300." Lovely subject matter I thought, hoping she was instructing a builder.

"Only 300?" replied Leonie, "I would have asked for 4, no 5 hundred.

"I should have darling, and you know what the stupid man said?"

"No tell me", Leonie asked, her voice full of excitement.

"Can I have a discount?"

"WHAT DID HE SAY???" Leonie was broadcasting to the entire bar now.

"HE ASKED FOR DISCOUNT" shouted Patrycja.

"I told him, put on your clothes and get out!"

The ladies then laughed hysterically, while I shifted uncomfortably on my stool, feeling the eyes of every person in the bar upon me. This was how they behaved before the cocktails arrived. Once they started drinking there was no stopping them.

In between spending vast amounts of time checking their smartphones, they occasionally spoke to each other. It would have been preferable if they'd stuck to reading messages on their phones.

"I wish my tits were big like yours" Patrycia to Leonie.

"Oh darling, I wish I had your stamina" Leonie replying to Patrycia, followed by much laughing.

"So Simon" Patrycia addressing me.

"You think you can handle two women at the same time?", again, much too loud.

"Well ladies, perhaps not on a Monday evening, especially after a couple of cocktails".

They then began whispering rapidly, I saw Patrycia shaking her head, but Leonie appeared insistent.

"Simon?" Leonie said this slowly, as if contemplating something of great importance. "Have you ever heard of the Love Palace parties?" My heart stopped at the mention of the place that had been mentioned to me by the French Inspector. I tried to remain calm and keep my voice steady "Love Palace? I can't say that I have. Is that a new club?"

Amsterdam is full of clubs that are like one direction (hopefully) famous for 5 minutes, then vanish without a trace.

"No it is not night club, you stupid man, why would she tell you about a night club?", interjected Patrycia, aggressively.

"Ok Patrycia, keep your tattoos on, I was just asking a question", I shot back at her. Leonie leant forward, her breasts pressed comfortably on my arm, and conspiratorially whispered, "Simon, the Love Palace parties are exclusive invitation only adult parties."

"The most exclusive adult parties in the Netherlands" whispered Patrycia in my ear, her perky breasts pressing against me as she said this.

"You need the approval of the Devil" said Patrycia, in tones of reverence.

"It's invitation only, and the Devil approves each person individually." The Devil again. Dmitry?

"What's so special about these parties then?" I asked, genuinely curious.

"You can have anything your heart desires at this party. No rules, society doesn't exist, nor law, only the rules of desire, passion, no limits at all." Leonie's eyes widened as she spoke, I could feel her excitement, and she pressed her fabulous breasts into me with each sentence. She then put her hands on my face and we kissed, tentatively at first, then with passion.

One of the bar men loudly cleared his throat. A subtle hint, that this kind of behavior was not really on in such a place. We parted.

"So where are these parties held?" I asked, recovering from the hot kiss we'd just had.

"That is secret!" cried Patrycia. "If you are approved, you will receive a text message on the day of the party. You'll be collected by car and taken directly to the party.

"What's the dress code?"

"Dress code is not important sweet thing", Leonie said this while stroking my leg. "Nice jeans Simon".

"Dress code" scoffed Patrycia,.

"Clothing is strictly optional" whispered Leonie sweetly, running her hands up my arm as she said this. By this time it was already almost 10. The girls were working at the strip bar that night, so naturally I settled the bill. We walked onto the Van Baerlestraat where the girls had their bikes parked. Patrycia, even though she was dressed in an excuse of a mini skirt, hopped onto her bike and waited for Leonie to give me a hot kiss goodbye. I even managed to get my hands under her top to sample her magnificent assets, before she cycled off in the direction of the Red Light District with Patrycia.

Upon getting home, I was faced with a dilemma; should I call the local policeman whose card I was given by Inspector Texier?

If I did, what I would tell him? Yes I'd been invited to a Love Palace party, but had so little info, I really didn't have anything worth telling. I decided not to contact him until I at least knew if I'd been accepted to the party and once I knew where it would be held.

# JULY 16TH

While picking out another beautiful suit for the day, I watched AT5, the local Amsterdam cable news station. Well, should say listened to it while getting ready. I'd been out running, doing interval training. This in spite of waking up with a slight headache after getting through several cocktails with the girls the previous evening.

Those ladies were definitely hardcore, in more ways than one. They threw cocktails down their neck as if prohibition were coming into law the next morning, and yet were still able to cycle off to work for another night of having their breasts licked. Incredible.

While making a yoghurt and forest fruit shake in the blender for breakfast, heard the news about another gangland shooting and drug rip in Amsterdam. Apparently, over a 100 rounds were fired with semi-automatic weapons into a car leaving one dead and two wounded. The Police refused to divulge if anything was taken, but there was talk of drugs and/or money being involved in the incident.

After another day of listening to Koen drone on about his new car, I decided it was time to put him in his place.

Once I got home, I set the wheels in motion. A former hobby of mine, that I went on to get bored of, was photography. I'd taken quite a few photos in my time of various friends and colleagues, which I still had stored on my home computer system. I found a pretty good photo of Koen and then set about creating a dating profile for him on an Expat dating site.

There's a site that I'd used myself once, during a bleak period following another short lived fling with the aforementioned Lucy. Dating sites are notorious for people stretching the truth. Nothing is ever what it seems to be on the profiles, which are created by a mixture of psychopaths, liars, sex addicts and a smattering of people who are too lazy or just too plain anti-social to meet people any other way. Far it be from me however, to generalise. I set about creating a suitable dating profile for Koen. As part of a team building exercise, we'd once visited a Spa Hotel, and I had several photos of him in his swimming trunks.

I built a profile which I linked to a disposable email address I'd created for it. However, I made sure to use his real name.

I added several photos and then added the following info.

About me:

Successful, Director at a leading Management Consultancy

Firm.

About my match:

Must have boobies that when she is sitting down will touch the table. They must be attention grabbers. My ideal woman will have nothing more than high school education and will not have any strong opinions on politics, current affairs and hobbies that go beyond shopping and activities that enhance her looks such as lots of physical exercise.

Interests:

My interests are my new BMW 5 series.

Characteristics:

Am considerably overpaid.

I laughed to myself as I wrote this. I was in a fabulous mood for the rest of the evening, and spent several hours destroying my online enemies during an extended game of Call of Duty.

# JULY 17TH

I woke up in a great mood. Irina had messaged me several times apologising for overreacting, however, I decided not to bother replying for now. I also had more hate mail from Lucy, whose anger knew no bounds.

At work, I was called into Koen's office.

"Simon, take a look at this". He pointed at his computer screen that was on his Facebook page.

"I don't know what's happening but I've had five hot looking women contact me today with friend requests." Startled, I had to agree that based on the profile photos, the women who had contacted him were indeed hot.

"Have you changed your profile picture? What's behind this sudden interest in you from the ladies?" I asked, knowing full well that this was obviously related to the dating profile I'd created for him.

"No idea, but I need to be careful as Ronja (his girlfriend) might start asking questions if she starts seeing hot ladies in my friend list."

I advised him not to worry about it. I'd only met Ronja a couple of times and she didn't seem to be the kind of person that spent vast amounts of time with social media. She had her hands full with two kids under the age of five. He agreed and said that she very rarely, if ever, used Facebook so he could probably get away with adding them as friends. After all, it's not as if he was doing anything wrong, just being sociable and making new virtual friends.

I left his office smiling. Step 2 of my 3 point plan was in place. I had to admit being surprised at how quickly he'd received responses though. At least two of the girls making friend requests with him were Russian, my favorites.

Anna had returned from a short business trip to Romania. We agreed to meet for a drink that evening, with Nat who was also coming along. Richard was off sick from work again. I gave him a call but received no response. I wondered what the hell he was up to. He'd been acting suspiciously lately, and his sudden newly acquired wealth was causing me some concern, but sadly as it later transpired, not enough to make me change the events that would occur.

# JULY 18$^{TH}$

In the previous evening, I had a civilized evening with Anna and Nat, who took great pleasure in describing to her the look of shock on my face as Irina let herself in to my apartment with a set of keys. Anna, thought this was hilarious, he knowing my views on having people entering my island.

"That was bloody quick Simon, giving her a set of keys"

"I did not give her permission to use them, nor did I give her a spare set. She simply helped herself to the spare keys which I had in a drawer in the spare room." As I said this, it suddenly occurred to me how odd that sounded.

"So you're saying she just went through your stuff till she found your keys? Aren't you worried what else she might have looked at?", asked Nat, with genuine concern in his voice.

"Come on guys, I know it doesn't sound good, but it's not as bad as it appears. I was still asleep in bed and she wanted to surprise me with a cooked breakfast. My main keys were in my coat pocket, she didn't want to wake me, so searched until she found a set of keys."

I could see by the expressions on their faces that neither Anna nor Nat were convinced, but we moved on from that and actually had a pleasant evening.

That evening, I had nothing in particular planned. I'd half considered paying Leonie a visit at work but decided that seeing multiple guys feasting on her wouldn't be ideal. With these thoughts in my mind I walked back to my apartment, around 8 pm, having attended a late conference call with colleagues in the US.

It was a beautiful evening and with my mind full of the potential joys of Leonie, I barely noticed the odd noise behind me as I walked. Some sixth sense must have kicked in, because I suddenly turned round and behind me was a man about my height, wearing a heavy black coat, which in itself was unusual due to the hot weather. He had one leg, the other was clearly artificial. He moved towards me with a limp. Speaking with what appeared to be a Russian accent, but in flawless English

"Simon Woolcot, we'd like to speak with you". My brain wondered what he meant by we, as he appeared to be alone. My question was answered when out of a van that was parked almost in front of my building stepped a muscular looking large guy, with a shaven head, dressed completely in black with eyes that looked like a gateway to Hell.

"Meet my friend, we shall call him Norman. He and I work

for a certain person, whose property you have infringed upon. We are here to ask you to desist from any contact with the said person, who you know as Natasha."

There was something in the tone of this voice, that while on the surface was polite, clearly contained not so hidden promises of unpleasant things to come, if I failed to heed his advice. Alarmed, I did my best attempt to convince them that it was all a misunderstanding.

"Listen, what shall I call you?" The one legged man, whose eyes never left me for a second suggested that I call him Norman.

"Norman? So you're both called Norman?"

"Yes, is that a problem?", replied the other Norman, the larger, shaven headed human pit bull.

"No, no problem at all"

"Listen chaps, we have a misunderstanding. Irina, my girlfriend, the love of my life actually, is good friends with Natasha and I just happened to be with Irina seeing as how she's such good friends". At this, the one legged Norman raised his hand, gesturing for me to stop talking.

"It will be good for your health, if you spend time with Irina and stay away from Natasha. It would be unfortunate to have to damage such a beautiful suit." As he said this he ran his hand upwards across my jacket up to my neck, where his hand suddenly, briefly, for no more than a couple of seconds grabbed my throat with surprising speed and strength. He stopped as quickly as he'd began, leaving me coughing and rubbing my throat in pain.

"We wish you a pleasant evening Simon, I hope we have no cause to visit you again. I love the outfit." With that they both got into the van and drove away.

# BOOK 5, THE BOOK OF SLOTH

# TIPS FROM THE AMSTERDAM MOUSE CATCHER GENERAL

One normally peaceful man, who has often been compared with Mandela, the Dalai Lama and Ghandi driven to fight a war with invaders.

The comparison with the above figures is usually along the lines of "you are so annoying that even Ghandi would lose his patience and punch you."

For the second night running I was able to set a trap and kill another mouse. Even if you don't see mouse droppings anywhere, in Amsterdam that doesn't mean that you don't have them. If you live in an old building in Amsterdam the chances are that your apartment has unwanted late night visitors.

Some tips for checking if you have mice in your apartment:

If you have a DVR recorder check the programs that have been recorded. If any documentaries have been recorded with titles such as the history of cheese, the peanut butter chronicles or the great cheeses of France you probably have mice.

Forget buying crappy 1 Euro wooden mouse traps. Baby mice are taught by their parents how to dodge those things as soon as they can walk. As the local mice are used to Dutch mouse traps, buy traps from different countries which they are unlikely to have seen.

Tips on bait to tempt mice. If you live in Amsterdam South use parmesan cheese or brie,; if you live in Amsterdam Southeast use something from a burger bar; if you live in Amsterdam East use kebab meat and in Amsterdam West, bits of food from any take away.

# JULY 19TH

Following my encounter with the two Normans I had a disturbed and restless night, leaping awake with a start, at every noise that appeared to be coming from within my apartment. Have you ever lay awake at night and listened, really listened to the strange noises? I figured that the ghosts of mice, that I'd recently slaughtered with the aide of some ingenious traps I'd ordered from the UK were lurching around, mousetrap on neck, coming to get me.

I was seriously worried. What was happening to me? To my perfect life? Mad women with GHB and now one legged Russian hit men? After hours of deliberation, in the early hours of the morning, I made a decision on what I needed to do.

I was too shaken up by my encounter with the Normans to go to work. I called in sick and then managed to sleep for several hours. It was after 11 in the morning when I finally got out of bed. Normally, I would have gone for a run, but had no wish to leave the apartment, lest another encounter with the one legged man and his human pit bull should occur.

Did some work from home, then jumped on the PlayStation to help calm my nerves. Time flew, then I made the call I was dreading but that I knew was necessary.

"Irina, I'd like you to come back, bring your stuff with you and you're welcome to stay as long as you wish". Shocked noises on the other end of the line.

"What? Are you serious? But Why?". Time to lie now

"The truth is that not having you around, made me realise how much I missed you. I like waking up with you next to me, and it's not just about sex".

"Oh Simon, I always hoped you'd say this, I can't believe it. You want me to move in with you?" How many times do I need to say it? I wondered, more than a little irritated. Doing my best to keep my voice slushy and romantic. "Yes Irina, I need you".

A sob from Irina.

"When do you want me to move in?"

"No time like the present, how about this evening?", I asked, knowing that somehow, I'd regret this.

# JULY 20TH

Another Saturday morning, with the lovely Irina. I was exhausted, but not for the reasons that you're thinking. She arrived, with enough suitcases to open her own travel shop. It took ages to unpack her stuff and make room in my own wardrobe space.

It had been years since I'd last lived with a woman. Yes, my motives for her moving in weren't entirely honorable. The way I figure it is that if I'm cooped up with Irina, Dmitry and his goons are likely to leave me in peace. I have no interest in Natasha, and why anyone would think otherwise was beyond me, however better safe than sorry.

She thinks that I can't live without her, I know that unless I convince interested parties that she is the center of my attention, I really won't be able to live, period.

There are definite pluses and minuses related to having someone living on Woolcot island.

Pluses:

- Sex on Tap
- Cooked breakfast, lunch and dinner
- Hot semi-naked body wandering around the apartment, ready and willing for sex, but I guess I covered that already.
- Minus points:
- Female stuff filling up all of my bathroom cabinets. Depilation cream, make up pads, make up remover, tampons!
- Enough hair products to burn a hole in the ozone layer directly above my building.
- Less available time for PlayStation. Not that playing was verboten, but lots of rolling of eyes, sighs and looks of displeasure appeared on her face whenever the subject came up.
- Plants! Bloody plants. What is it with women and plants? I don't want to share my oxygen with these things. She'd only been in the apartment for 5 minutes and there are already little flies buzzing around. Thanks Irina.

On Saturday I was supposed to be meeting Anna for lunch. While Irina went shopping, I spent some quality time on the PS3.

I was so engrossed in a game of tennis that I completely forgot the time, leading to an angry call from Anna, thanking me for standing her up. I let her call go to voicemail and continued with my game.

Irina was in a fabulous mood, mine was not so good, but I put on an Oscar winning performance of a man who was over the moon with his new live-in lover.

"It's beautiful weather outside Simon, why we no go out?" she asked, following a healthy tuna salad.

"Honey, if you want to go out, go for it. I'm not in the mood and will stay here" I said this hoping it would be the end of the discussion.

"Mood? What mood. We go out, we enjoy the sun, we" "Listen, I don't want to go out, so let's not waste each others time discussing it ok?" Usually, this would have led to a heated debate, but obviously not wishing to rock the boat, Irina let the subject lie, and we spent the rest of the day on the sofa.

# I AM NOT AN AMSTERDAM ELITIST

Some misguided individuals, accuse me of having lost touch with my roots. They say, Shallow Man, you live in an apartment in the Pijp area of Amsterdam paid for by your organisation. You eat in Michelin star restaurants, wear bespoke suits and shoes, you wear designer clothes and use luxury lotions and aftershave; in short, they accuse me of being out of touch with my fellow man.

Well I couldn't disagree more with such assertions and as proof of this I call forward the following exhibits for consideration by an impartial and unbiased jury of my peers.

**Exhibit 1.**

I walk to my local Supermarket. I even take time to pass through the "things to put on bread" section. There is even peanut butter in my pantry.

**Exhibit 2**

In spite of hating the patronising TV commercials for the Albert Hein supermarket that appear to assume that all of their customers are sad, brain dead, hopeless, simple minded, jelly eating morons with a mental age of ten or less, I still shop there. That's in spite of all fruit purchased there self destructing almost on the way home from the supermarket. If you wish to aid the fruit fly Eco system, purchase fruit from AH and leave it unattended in your apartment, penthouse or palace for a few hours. I guarantee that fruit flies will be holding orgies and dogging events in your very own fruit bowl and their population will multiply.

**Exhibit 3**

I take my own clothes to the dry cleaners and collect them myself.

**Exhibit 4**

I call my cleaner by his first name.

**Exhibit 5**

I use public transport., even the metro from Amstel to Arena, and share my space with people eating fast food with their mouths open. All within sight and smell of the Shallow Man and I don't complain.

**Exhibit 6**

I actually am on a first name basis with the receptionists in my company. That they are blond and have rather large breasts is purely coincidental.

**Exhibit 7**

I always leave a 10% tip at restaurants and bars. The Shallow Man was a student once, and understands how appalling it is to have to serve the general public.

I hope the above will prove once and for all that I am and remain a man of the people.
I need to get back to GTA five. Hou Je Bek.

# JULY 21ST

Spent most of the day repeating a familiar pattern with Irina. Intense sex, breakfast, more sex followed by lunch. We then spent some time going through my collection of quality pornography, which of course led to more sex.

My phone vibrated several times with various messages. Each time I reached for it, Irina would observe me closely and then immediately ask Wwho was that from? Who is texting you?"

I'd received the usual annoying Facebook updates. A friend of a friend of a distant friend playing with a kitten. A woman standing in front of a fruit stall pointing at it as if it were the last seller of fruit on the planet. "Wow, look at me, I've discovered a place where they sell fruit!"

Leonie sent me a text message that was too filthy to repeat here. It involved doing various things to her, followed by massaging her breasts in a new, unusual and rather messy way. Lovely girl.

In the interests of transparency, I showed Irina the message. "What a filthy bitch! Who she think she is?" Making a grab for my phone.

Me: "What are you doing?"

Irina: "I want to delete her from your contacts. You should have nothing to do with such a whore". I'd managed to hang on to the phone and put it in the pocket of the reassuringly expensive McGregor dressing gown I was wearing.

"Irina, I've been honest with you and shown you the message. I decide what gets deleted from my phone, not you."

Her eyes tearing up, "Yes but we live together no? You shouldn't keep in contact with such a whore. Why you want to keep in contact?" Again, decided honesty was the best policy.

"Actually, I need her number as she's going to get me in to the next Love Palace party." With that Irena stood up and marched upstairs to the bedroom, cursing at me in Russian as she left. Following her I asked, "What the hell is wrong now?" Her eyes narrow and full of rage, speaking in a barely audible tone. "Love Palace, you are invited to fucking Love Palace". "Yes, not bad eh, it's supposed to be quite exclusive", I responded happily. With that she picked up a glass of water that was on the bedside cabinet and hurled it at my head. Managing to dodge it just in time, I watched as it shattered into pieces against the wall.

"Was that really necessary Irina? I hope you know that you're cleaning that up." I said as I pointed to the mess of broken glass all over the floor.

"Do you know what the Love Palace is? Do you?" she asked breathing heavily.

"Yes of course, it's a kind of erotic party where anything goes. I'd like to check it out, just for the experience, and actually, I'd like you come with me". She remained silent for awhile, sat on the bed, and with her head in her hands said, "You will never get me to go to such a place, never". I was confused.

"But we've been to swinger clubs before, what's the difference?"

"There's a big difference Simon, that you really don't want to find out. But you know, if you want to go, then go. I will not stop you. It's your life". With that, all of the energy went out of her, and she curled up on the bed in the fetal position where she remained for some time.

Relieved, I grabbed the opportunity for some PlayStation time and even cleaned up the broken glass before doing so.

# TALES FROM THE AMSTERDAM CULTURAL SCENE

As a fully rounded mature forty something male with a broad appreciation of the performing arts, I and a couple of fellow culture vultures decided to partake in an evening of performance art.

Upon arriving and recognising us as obvious experts in our field a helpful gentleman with an east European accent ushered us past the readers of the Telegraaf, the Dutch equivalent of the Sun newspaper. We passed a football supporting mob elegantly dressed in football shirts that cost as much as a week of their income and the nervous hyena- like giggles of a group of women with bad hair, jeans (naturally) and the smell of cheap cigarettes. Nearby, trying to get the girls' attention was a group of seedy looking men with slicked back hair and cheap suits, obviously local Makkelaars/Estate Agents.

Taking us to a "VIP" corner, i.e. we will milk you like a Gold Digger ploughing her way through the bank account of her footballer boyfriend, he politely asked us "what you drink gentlemen?" having decided on a bottle of eye wateringly expensive Vodka, our host explained the origins of that evening's performing artists.

"We have many pretty girl, Estonian, Bulgarian, Greek, Serbian, Italian". As he imparted this information with the excitement of a Romanian pick pocket at a music festival, the Vodka was brought to our table by an older, slightly overweight woman with the kind of face that could sour milk and bring terror to the hearts of pit bulls. She slammed the Vodka on the table along with some glasses and stalked off foul temperedly back from whence she came.

Our genial and excitable host continued with his trip around the world of the origins of his performers. "You like a bit of fat on a woman? We have British girls. You like a woman that talks too loud and has badly cut hair? We have Dutch girls. You like a woman that looks like she was a sparring partner for Mike Tyson? We have Polish girls. You like a woman with a bad attitude and short temper?" " You have French girls?" I asked knowing what was coming next. "Oh yes we have a French girl working she is beautiful" as he said this, he gestured with his hand and knocked over the bottle of Vodka which was in an ice bucket whose contents fell on my beautifully made bespoke mohair trousers. "Can you get me a serviette?" I asked.

"Serviette? Serviette?" He asked his voice rising. "I'm so sorry sir we don't have any Russian girls working here tonight. (Soviets)

# BOOK 6, THE BOOK OF PRIDE

# JULY 22ND

Pride is a funny thing. In the right circumstances it can lead to bold decision making. However, applied in the wrong situation, it can be deadly.

Another day at work. Sat in a meeting with our HR team who were presenting the new process for carrying out staff appraisals. This was something that often annoyed the hell out of me. At least every 2 to 3 years, our HR team present the latest process for evaluating staff. Each time they do this, it's presented by a near hysterical HR type, who acts as if they've been to Mount Sinai and have returned with the new HR processes handed personally to them by God himself.

The upshot of this is that just as managers and team members become used to the way of setting goals and managing the year end process, these are changed completely. This has led to a level of cynicism that is shared by Partners, management and employees alike.

The reality is that all of the whizz-bang software and rainforests volume of paper to support the process, still can't prevent appraisals being incredibly subjective. The old boy/girl network still very much exists and often the people who go on to senior management do so, not so much by merit, but through a combination of knowing the right people and making the correct noises at the opportune time. Originality and independence are desired but not expected to be used at McCulloch. Kiss arse, wine and dine with the right people and you'll be on the stairway to heaven. It certainly worked for me.

Had a disturbing conversation with Koen, the serpent. If you were to throw that man out of a moving plane, he'd land in an open top truck full of money and semi-naked playboy models.

Incredibly, my dating agency prank had backfired. Not only had he been contacted by numerous women, who were actually looking for a man that wants a women with no ambition or opinions, the snake had actually met up with and shagged one, as well. He showed me some compromising photos that he'd taken with his smartphone of her in various poses and positions, and she was a talented lady indeed.

"Her name is Kristina, she's from Latvia, isn't she beautiful?" He said so excited that I was afraid he was going to cum in his pants right there.

"She's hot, I can't believe you met up with her", I said bitterly.

"Not only is she hot, she's as dumb as the backend of a cow!"

That's an old Dutch saying apparently. He continued.

"I never had sex like it. What a woman. Well girl, she's 22". Twenty bloody two. I couldn't believe it.

"I love the Internet, apparently my profile has become active on a dating site. I didn't create it, perhaps one of my friends did it as a joke, but whoever it was I'm grateful.", laughed the snake, formerly know as Koen. Disgusted I returned to my desk.

Richard was still AWOL from work. I'd left countless messages for him and he'd not bothered to reply until late last night, while I was busy being worked out on by Irina. Being the mature chap that I am, I ignored his call and several others made by him at unsociable times during the night. I was severely pissed off with him now and to make things worse, Marcie, his big and tough better half had called me at work, demanding to meet up that evening, which was all that I needed. I tried calling him back in the morning, but no response.

I headed over to Marcie and Richard's place in the Jordaan neighbourhood. Marcie was some kind of bureaucrat for Amsterdam city council, so obviously Richard brought in the lion's share of the income. They lived in a feminine apartment, full of flowers, photos of family, and fluffy cushions on the Prinsengracht.

As I entered the apartment, Marcie, who was a big woman, greeted me with a slap in the face that had my ears ringing and me checking that all of my teeth were still intact afterwards.

"Marcie, what the fuck was that for?", I backed away from her towards the door.

"That was a preview of what's going to happen to you if I think you're lying to me, Woolcot.", she shouted with tears in her eyes. She looked as if she'd been crying and hadn't had much sleep.

"Look calm down, why would I lie to you? What about? I don't know anything". She started to raise her hand again and I instinctively threw my hands in front of my face. She pointed towards a room that I knew Richard used as his office and place to watch pornography in private.

"Take a look in his bolt hole then tell me that you don't know anything", she said with a tone of pure contempt in her voice.

She waited in the living room as I entered his room, which was just large enough to fit a single desk, chair and some shelves that were full of various books on computer programming and computer security. In a past life, he was a talented programmer and had worked for our IT Risk Management business, advising organisations on how best to protect themselves from being hacked into by spotty teenagers and organized crime gangs.

The room looked as if a tornado had been through it. Books and papers were scattered everywhere. I wondered what Marcie wanted me to see, which was the point of the exercise, but then I saw it. On the floor next to a pile of overturned books and papers was an open metal briefcase, which was full of money, and lots of it.

I approached Marcie, who had calmed down and was sobbing quietly to herself.

"You've seen it? and there's much more of it. I've found over 40,000 Euros in cash hidden all over the apartment. I only started looking because I became suspicious with him not coming home for two nights in a row now." She was crying as she said this, and then with a look of pure hatred pointed a fat finger at me.

"Whenever he's in trouble, you're never far behind, it's been that way for as long I've known the two of you, and he tells me it was the same when you were growing up together in London as well. So for once in your shallow life, (shallow!) I want you to tell me the truth, what's going on?"

I proceeded to tell her what I knew. About the night at the live sex show and later his cryptic references to doing a deal with the Devil. I asked her if she hadn't wondered how he could afford a Hublot watch and expensive new clothes, but he'd kept the watch hidden from her and must have changed it when he came home.

From her side she told me that since the night at the sex show, he regularly worked late. He'd told her that he was doing some freelance IT security work on the side for a Russian businessman called Dmitry and that he paid him very well, in cash, but of course she wasn't expecting to see piles of cash lying around.

"What do you think I should do?"

"I suggest that you stay calm Marcie, there's no point in worrying about things you don't know. I'll get in touch with some of the guys to see if they've heard from him and I'll keep calling him as well."

Marcie had tried contacting him in the last couple of days but to no avail. I said I'd try my best and let her know. As I left their apartment, she called after me.

"I'm so worried Simon, should I call the Police?"

"No, it's too soon, he's a grown man, I'm sure he'll resurface soon". Indeed he did, but not in the way we were expecting.

The Shallow Man, being the highly eligible man about Amsterdam that he his, often finds himself in varying relationships at various stages. Depending on how new or how dreadfully old a relationship is, also taking into account the usual cycle of 1st date excitement, mid relationship tedium, and end of relationship wailing and gnashing of teeth, it's important that the man or indeed woman about town has a suitable portfolio of restaurants in which to play out these stages of the eternal struggle.
To help with this challenge I've developed the following guide.

**1st dates**

You can tell a lot about the first date partner and where to take them for dinner based largely on what he/she was drinking the first time you met. If you're one of the rare individuals who meets new dates while both of you are stone cold sober, I take my hat off to you sir or madam, for you are indeed a silver tongued bar steward.

To save time I'll assume that we are talking about women, but the same can apply to men too.

Now if you did meet in an environment where alcohol was involved try and remember, if you can, what was she drinking? If it was wine then she is highly likely to have a reasonable palate which means you should take her to a place where the food is good and reasonably priced. If she was drinking beer, then what are you doing going on a date with her? Ok, assuming that she is incredibly hot, which she'd need to be for justifying dating a beer drinker, the other thing to consider is was she smoking? If the answer is yes and she is Dutch, you can take her to an Eetcafe. There's no point wasting money on fine dining for a smoking beer drinker. FEBO a place where food is sold out compartments in the wall is also an option. A couple of croquettes, washed down with beer then straight to bed.

For a woman that drinks Wine and doesn't smoke, I recommend one of the following:
The La Vina Experience in the Maasstraat

La Vina is a reasonably priced diamond hidden in a coal pile of mediocrity that is the Amsterdam restaurant scene. They have superb fine dining, with simple well flavored dishes, an excellent wine list and friendly, genuinely warm service with a smile. It's so reasonably priced that even if you fail to achieve your primary goal you won't wake up the following morning with a financial hangover.

My next first date recommendation is the superb Brasserie Van Baerle

This is another one of those hidden gems in Amsterdam. They specialise in simple classic French food, great wine, outstanding quality meat, service and a very nice decor. Ideal if you want to impress the knickers or boxer shorts of your date for the evening.

**Mid-relationship dating**

It eventually happens to all of us, yes even I the Shallow Man reach the stage in a relationship where birthdays, or horror of horrors anniversaries or that dire commercial event developed solely to torment men, Valentine's Day occurs. Before I go further, I'd like to put a request to womanhood in general; please don't ask your partner if they remember the date when you first met. How in the name of Bob Marley are we supposed to know such a thing?

I digress, so on with the advice. So the dreaded point arrives when you have to celebrate "something". Society expects you to rise to the occasion, so like a performing lion in a circus the whip is cracked and you roar into action.

If you really want to impress not only your partner but their respective parents, relatives, co-workers, parents and friends of co-workers, mistresses and partners of complete strangers who happen to shop in the local Albert Hein or sit next to you at the local Hairdresser, take them to Ciel Bleu.

The Shallow Man is not easily impressed, and yet I must say that every time I visit this place it genuinely takes my breath away. From the moment you arrive you are entering a portal to another planet and that planet is called service. The food is on another level, nothing that is served vaguely resembles how your mind expects it to be. The amuses are better than the main courses in 90% of restaurants I've ever been to.

The service is as structured, coordinated and choreographed as the Bolshoi Ballet, Romeo and Juliet the Opera and Michael Jackson's Thriller. Food is served simultaneously to both parties. Glasses of wine are topped up by a restaurant service team that are slicker than a snake in a barrel of oil. It's fine dining in a different galaxy. If Ciel Bleu were a woman, I'd marry her.

# BOOK 7, THE BOOK OF WRATH

# JULY 23RD

Another restless night. Tried calling Richard, multiple times, but no answer. Woke up to the smell of fresh croissants; Irina had popped out to the bakers on the corner of Ferdinand Bolstraat and was already fully dressed and ready for work. She continued to amaze me as in all the time that I'd known her, I'd still yet to see her put her hands in her pocket and pay for anything.

Hopped into my Uber taxi, which this morning was an Audi A8, nicely air-conditioned and a smooth ride to work. After a morning of death by PowerPoint from a sweating, stuttering Partner of McCulloch on our sustainability strategy, I was in serious need of some fresh air.

I was just walking out of the building when I was shocked to see Claudine, waiting for someone in our reception area.

"Simon, so good to see you" she cried in her sing song French accent and threw her arms around me. Releasing myself from her embrace which I did not return,

"Claudine what are you doing here?" Her face suddenly changed.

"Are you not pleased to see me Simon?", correctly reading my distaste in seeing her here unannounced.

"Who are you here to see?", ignoring her question.

"Oh, you really are not happy to see me, and I thought that we always got on so well. Very well. I'm here to see the Head of your organization's Telecoms consulting practice, to see if we can work together. I'm pleased to see you, I was going to call you and ask you to join me for dinner this evening at Ciel Bleu, which I know you like."

I laughed at this and then raising the temperature a little and ignoring the advice of the French Police asked her:

"So how's Daniela? Is she back at work?" Her face reddened at this and her body suddenly went tense, looking at me as if I were being served on a plate for her consumption.

"You silly boy, why are you asking this? You know that she left and never returned, why would I know where she is?". Ignoring this I pressed on.

"Claudine, I won't be joining you for dinner, as I've only eaten with you twice, and on both occasions I've woken up in a terrible state the next day, not knowing what the hell happened." She giggled, sexily.

"Well you silly boy, you shouldn't drink so much. You English and your drink, you just have to learn when to say no."

"Which is what I'm doing right now. No Claudine, I don't want to have dinner with you this evening, nor any other time. Have a good day". With that I walked off, shaking off the look of indignation on her face. She muttered something in French after me, and I'm sure that I heard the word diable. Wish I'd paid more attention at school in French class; c'est la vie.

I was looking forward to having dinner with Irina that evening, she'd even called me and asked what time I'd be home so she could prepare it on time. She wouldn't tell me what she was cooking but said it would be a surprise.

I arrived in the apartment with high expectations and was surprised; not only was there no smell of cooking, but no sign of Irina either.

The kitchen was spotlessly clean, with no sign of any food having been prepared there today at all. Something then occurred to me, my PS3 was missing. I looked around to see if anything else had been taken and then in the walk in wardrobe, my suits, my beautiful tailor made suits had been thrown in a heap on the floor and someone had slashed them with a knife. My Prince of Wales Scabal, my two piece black suit, my favorite blue one was destroyed as well. There was thousands of Euros worth of damage done to suits and shirts as well, and then, almost as bad, the scumbags had taken a knife to some of my boots and shoes as well. My God!

I sat on the floor in shock, not knowing what to do. Where was Irina? I called her but she didn't respond. I then called Anna, who said she'd be with me as soon as possible. I decided to go upstairs to the bedroom to lie down; I was so shocked. On the pillow was a single sheet of paper.

Simon,

How are you? Are you surprised? By now you would have seen the mess that I've made of the things you love the most, your things, your possessions. How is my English Simon? Is it good enough for you? You think it's funny to laugh at the way I speak, just because I am not a native speaker, you think it's ok to write, making fun of my grammar. That's what you think isn't it?
You always think of yourself as being so clever, don't you Shallow Man. That's what they call you, and I think it's a very good name for you. You were careless!
All those years in IT and yet you use Scabal223 (the number of the street you live on) as a password! How stupid are you. So yes

shallow man, I know all your dirty secrets. I read your diary. I know about Leonie, and Claudine and how you used me. Yes used me because you were afraid!
What a coward you are, you're not a man, you're still a boy. So I took the PlayStation and your games, and destroyed some of your suits. Lucky for you that some are in the dry cleaners or I would have destroyed them too. You bastard. I hate you for breaking my heart. You never told me you loved me, but I always hoped, but you don't want love do you? No the Shallow Man is an island. Then fine, rot on your island alone!

You will never see me again. For years to come, remember what I did to you, I HATE YOU.

# JULY 24TH

I'm devastated, a ruin, a shadow of my former self. Anna came round last night and I cried, yes the Shallow Man cried like a baby and I don't know if it was for the loss of the suits and the PS3 or if I had feelings for Irina after all. Anna didn't gloat, she consoled me as best she could and we fell asleep in each others arms on the sofa.

We woke up around 1 am and I walked her home. She'd asked if I'd call the Police but then what could they do? The damage was done. Somehow, I had to pull myself together and get to work. I'd tried calling Irina but of course no response.

While I sat in the back of my taxi on the way to work, there was more disturbing news on the radio about the escalating gangland war that was going on. This time there had been a shooting incident in the Rivierenbuurt, uncomfortably close to where I lived. There was also another story that happens a lot in Amsterdam. Dumb tourists, usually British, take way too many drugs then jump out of windows either onto passing pedestrians or into Canals. A body had been found in a canal and it suspected that it was another tourist, off his head on drugs that had done this.

My solution to the problem is simple, don't allow any British tourists under the age of 30 to stay in any rooms above the first floor, problem solved.

I arrived in the office to be greeted by a security guard. He asked me to hand over my card and then escorted me to a meeting room where waiting for me was Jasper, the head of our HR team and Koen.

Jasper asked me to take a seat.

"Simon, we've had some disturbing news about you that we are duty bound to investigate. We've had a report from a confidential source that you have instigated a campaign of harassment against a colleague." What in the name of Bob Marley was going on?

"I have no idea what this is about." I replied honestly.

"BULLSHIT" cried Koen, take a look at this then." There was a printout of various emails on the table and as I read the first one, I realized what had happened. Irina, in her mad rage and logged on to my home computer, had sent messages to Koen's partner, from my email address, telling her about his rendezvous with the Latvian and to check out his Facebook profile.

"You bastard, how could you do this to me?" cried Koen, who also looked as if he hadn't slept.

"Koen, calm down, this will be investigated" said Jasper, then looking at me he handed over a letter which told me that I was suspended on full pay until the outcome of an investigation.

"Surely this a private matter between two friends" I said hoping this would help me some how. "Friends?" ,laughed Koen, "This is how you treat friends?"

Jasper, then told me the bad news, which was that the emails had been sent from my work address. I forgot that we had webmail access from home, that I sometimes used from my home computer. Irina really had stuck the knife into me good and proper.

In front of all of my colleagues, I was escorted by the security guard out of the building.

# JULY 25TH

So after 18 years loyal service to the company, I was facing a gross misconduct charge. What I should have been doing was hiring myself a lawyer, instead I went feeling sorry for myself to the Conservatorium Hotel and decided to have an early liquid lunch. I ordered a glass of champagne, the first of many. I ended up merry as a ticket tout selling tickets to One Direction fans and staggered home.

Had a few missed calls from an unknown number and a message from Leonie that I didn't bother reading.

Woke up the next morning with a splitting headache and the sound of the door bell ringing. I reached for the intercom.

A female voice. "Open the door Simon, it's me, Lucy". Shocked, that she even knew where I lived, I let her in. So there she was, my poison twin, the woman who had caused me so many problems in the past and yet, within seconds we were kissing with a passion so intense I was afraid that we'd set the apartment on fire.

Later, as we lay next to each in bed, I told her the pitiful story about Irina. Lucy was in Amsterdam from Australia for a week and a half to attend a planned conference at the RAI convention center and had deliberately arrived a few days early so that she would have time to acclimatize and of course catch up with me.

"What would you have done if a woman had answered the door?" shrugging her shoulders.

"I'd have invited myself in and beaten her to death, then I would have waited for you and fucked you to an early grave." That was the Lucy I knew and feared.

"You know you deserve what happened to you? I read what you wrote about me." "What? You mean she mailed a copy to you?"

"Yes she did, she's quite a woman that Irina, I quite like her. She did almost exactly what I would have in her situation. So what hurt more? The loss of the PlayStation or the clothes? Wait, don't tell me, let me guess. It's the PlayStation, because…., it would have had the progress of the games you play saved on it. So even if you go out and buy a new one, you'll still have to start all games from the beginning." She was correct. She laughed as I confirmed this. Shallow Man.

"Aren't you worried about one thing? If she sent me a copy of the diary, who else has she sent it to, have you checked?" My heart stopped as she said this and I went to the computer and checked the logs. I could see that the diary had only been sent to

Lucy and no one else. That was at least something to be grateful for.

"So you let Claudine drug you? Same old Simon, being led by his cock as always." "Lucy, say whatever you like, I'm not going to argue with you, not today."

That evening we went for dinner at one of my favorite restaurants in Amsterdam, Jasper's. A delightful, fine dining experience at a reasonable price.

Lucy and I were civilised, discussed old times and avoided any discussion about the future as we both knew that we didn't have one together. When the bill arrived I whipped out my bank PIN card to pay the 180 Euros and was surprised when at the first attempt the transaction was declined as was on the second and the third.

Jasper, who I knew well was red faced and very politely tried to blame the machine. I reached for the Platinum card and the same thing occurred, transaction declined. The day before I'd paid for lunch in cash, this was the first time I'd used the cards since Irina. Damn. Lucy settled the bill and I rushed home to go online and check my bank balance.

What was clear was that in the days preceding her leaving, there had been five withdrawals of 1000 Euros each on my bank account. I usually didn't keep too much cash in my account but had neglected to transfer some money to my savings account. I called the bank credit card hotline and was told that there had been suspicious transactions on my card so they'd locked the account, pending verification with me. They had attempted to contact me via phone and email but I hadn't responded. The suspicious activity was that Irina had obviously also used my Platinum card to withdraw money from an ATM, something that I never do normally.

My PIN numbers were easy to find. As I hadn't expected anyone to go through my personal belongings I'd left the numbers for both my bank and Platinum card in a drawer. She had probably found these while she was looking for my keys.

When I looked back through the transactions she'd been taking money from my account since the 21st of July, so that means that she must have discovered my diary on the night of the 20th. This was why she was always awake and fully dressed in the morning. She'd been going to the local ATM while I was asleep, then returning my wallet and cards unnoticed.

This was financial rape. I'd been violated. Incredible. Enraged, I marched round to Irina's pokey apartment. I was pressing the door bell, when a man who identified himself as her landlord, let me in.

He was a fifty something, with grey thinning hair.

"You looking for Irina?", he said, in faltering English.

"I'd love to see her too. She's left here without paying her rent, taken all of her stuff and just upped and left."

I asked him if he had any idea where she'd moved to.

"If I knew that, I wouldn't be standing here would I?", he stated somewhat annoyed. "One of the neighbors saw her leaving in a van with a man with one leg. Any idea who that might be?" I responded in the negative and after exchanging numbers, he asked me to let him know if I hear from her, something which I told him would be highly unlikely.

# JULY 26TH

I spent a lot of time at the bank. Had my PIN and credit card frozen and ordered replacements. As this was going to take a few days, I withdrew 1,000 Euros in cash to tide me over until the replacements arrived. I'd need at least 500 as I'd received a cryptic message from Leonie that a car would be coming to collect me at 9 pm that evening to take me to the party and that I'd need to have the money ready.

I called the number of the policeman on the card given to me by Inspector Texier and told him that the Love Palace party was going ahead and when I was being collected.

Lucy had gone to work for the day and was going out with colleagues.

My mind ran over the previous day's events. I still couldn't believe it. Irina had stolen from me. Had she acted in anger having read the diary or was this her plan all along? I had a sick feeling in my stomach and spent the day feeling severe pain, anger and hatred for Irina that she'd do such a thing to me.

Had I treated her badly? I don't think so. We were never the committed couple in love. She knew I wasn't into commitment, we had specifically discussed precisely that. She had never paid any money for anything when we were together, I treated her like a princess and this is how she treats me. What a bitch!

Anna came round to see if I was ok. She'd heard via the rumor mill that as it couldn't be proven that I actually sent the messages to Koen's partner, that I was likely to be let off with a warning.

How I'd face Koen after that was something I didn't want to think about.

Anna, had been at my place for 20 minutes or so, we were seated opposite each other at the dining table.

"Simon, I'm going to say some things to you now that you might not want to hear. However, I'm going to ask you not to interrupt, but just listen to me ok?"

I agreed that I'd do as she asked.

"We've been friends a long time and I've watched how you live. I've seen you go from woman to woman to bar to woman. Your existence is pointless. It's shallow. You value the material things in life, fine clothes, furniture, expensive watches, but these Simon are just objects. It's as if a part of you has died, your love if that's the correct description. You love things, not people." I listened carefully for once and she continued.

"The situation you have with Irina, can't be justified by your behavior. There is no justification for her stealing from you, but, you put yourself in that situation." I was about to respond. "Remember your promise."

"You put yourself in that situation by valuing sex over love. Your criteria for the relationship that the two of you had, were purely physical. You had nothing in common at all, but that didn't matter, what was important was how good she was in bed. You've been so busy chasing after different women, that you've overlooked and missed out on happiness. The happiness you could have had with someone like me, who loves you not for how much you earn, or the clothes you wear, but for who you are underneath all of this shit." At that point, I glanced at my watch as the car that would be taking me to the Love Palace would be arriving soon and I had to get ready.

"Well Anna, thanks a lot for speaking so honestly. It was interesting. I'll definitely give it some thought." At this point she jumped off my dining table chair and shouted, "unglaublich, (unbelievable), you're incredible. You arrogant, idiot. You'll never learn, will you?" She was shouting now. With that she stormed out slamming the door. I seem to have a knack for pissing her off. Knowing that she'd calm down eventually, I waited anxiously for the car to take me to the party. It arrived 15 minutes earlier than planned. I handed over 500 Euros to the driver as agreed and sat for 20 minutes as he drove in the direction of Amstelveen, which is just outside Amsterdam. The car then turned round and we drove in the opposite direction until we arrived at Amsterdam South station.

"We need to get out here" said the driver gruffly in a non-descript accent.

We got out and walked through the station.

"Turn here, we go back". We walked back in the direction we came and almost bumped into two typically tall Dutchmen. We went outside and I jumped into the back of the car. The driver took off at some speed. After another 40 minutes we arrived at a set of gates. The driver pressed an intercom, said something and then they opened. We drove along a pathway up to a large driveway in which were parked a number of cars in front of a mansion.

"You go in", said the driver, which was one of the longest sentences I'd heard from him so far. I walked up the main doors of the house in front of which stood a couple of giants in black suits who were obviously security. I wasn't sure but think that I recognized one of the bouncers from the live sex show.

They opened the main door and in the distance I could hear the sound of music and people talking. I walked along a long corridor which ended at a large open plan room, full of people in various states of undress. There were perhaps 40 to 50 people, men and women who could have been in their sixties or as young as twenty something.

The room had sofas and fur rugs scattered around on which people were rolling around together. On the far side of the main room was a long table that was covered with glasses of champagne and wine. At the other end of the room was a DJ. Something that struck me was that all of the women wore masks but not the men. A masked lady wearing only fine lingerie approached me and gave me a glass of champagne. I politely refused and walked over to the main table where there were glasses of wine and champagne and helped myself to a glass of white wine. Following my experiences with Claudine, I didn't want to risk taking a glass that may have been drugged.

As I started drinking the wine, I felt a tap on my shoulder. Standing there in the skimpiest of underwear was Leonie. "Hi Simon, come with me please." I followed her out of the main room through another set of doors that led to a flight of stairs. We climbed them and entered a long and narrow room at the far end of which three thrones sat. Upon the one in the center, naked except for a pair of shoes, sat Claudine. Everything I'd suspected about her body was correct, it was toned and perfect. To her left sat an overweight, mean looking brute of a man and to her right sat one of the Normans, he with one leg.

"Welcome Simon, you've met Norman. To my left is Dmitry. He bellowed out something in Russian and out of an adjacent room, on hands and knees, with dog collars round their necks and led in on chains pulled by the other Norman were Daniela and Natasha. I turned to look at the door through which we'd come, where now stood one of the giants that were earlier at the front door.

"The girls were led to the feet of Claudine, where they kneeled before her. I looked in Daniela's eyes and saw nothing. No sign of recognition, she looked as if she were drugged.

"So Simon, why do you look so nervous? Relax, have a drink." One of the giants brought over a glass of champagne.

"Drink Simon, right now". I took a sip of the champagne.

"If you're waiting for the Police to arrive, you are wasting your time. They won't be coming here. My driver made sure that you lost them on the way here.

"Police, what police?" I lied.

"Oh Shallow Man. Irina was kind enough to send me a copy of your diary, we know everything." At this point Dmitry rose from his throne and without saying a word pointed at my glass of champagne and made a drinking motion. I drank some more. Claudine smiled at me.

"Don't look so concerned Simon. You are here, because every decision you've ever taken in your life has led up to this moment. Drink some more." Her voice was cold and stern. "What does one do with a shallow man? A man that in spite of his better instincts must follow the path of instant gratification, always." My head pounded, I felt very tired, her voice seemed to be coming from far away. She rose and walked slowly towards me. "You who would interfere with my property, my business, betray me and my friends." She pointed at Dmitry. "You must be taught a lesson."

The world went black.

# JULY 27TH

I awoke in a hospital bed. Sat next to the bed were Anna, Lucy and Koen. Anna left the room and arrived with a nurse. I could see that I was connected to an IV drip.

I fell asleep. Later when I woke up, Anna told me the bad news. "I'm sorry Simon, there's no other way of putting this, Richard is dead. His body was found in a canal in the Keizersgracht earlier this week. The Police think that he was tortured first then pumped full of drugs and either jumped or was pushed into the canal. They were here earlier and will come and speak to you later."

A policeman entered the room and told me the following.

Richard was working for Dmitry, who as well as controlling sex clubs and strip bars was quite a player in the Amsterdam underworld. Richard had been hacking into the computers and phones of the rivals of Dmitry and had given him a lot of useful information on the movements and plans of his rivals. Unfortunately, someone in Dmitry's organisation leaked this info to a rival gang and Richard was snatched and killed.

I was in complete and total shock. I was numb. He was my best friend, how could this happen? He'd tried to call me, could I have helped him? I bawled my eyes out like a newborn baby. Once I'd calmed down, he continued the tale. Claudine and Dmitry were part of the same organisation. She is Dmitry's cousin and is suspected of being involved in the abduction and trafficking of girls across Europe. Many girls end up working in various private bordellos in the Netherlands, a lucrative business.

The Love Palace party was raided by the Police, but Claudine got away. They were able to rescue a number of women that were reported missing, including Daniela. Claudine's whereabouts are unknown.

It turns out that Claudine's nickname in underworld circles is the Diable or simply the Devil. So the Devil really does wear Prada.

# ABOUT THE AUTHOR

Simon Woolcot is a privileged Expat who came to Amsterdam from London for a six month assignment and has remained for nine years. Planning is obviously not his strong point. He spends his time commenting on various aspects of life in Holland on the Amsterdam Confessions of a Shallow Man Blog: amsterdamshallowman.com

Made in the USA
San Bernardino, CA
19 January 2014